Lady Violet Greville

Creatures of Clay

Vol. III

Lady Violet Greville

Creatures of Clay
Vol. III

ISBN/EAN: 9783337065355

Printed in Europe, USA, Canada, Australia, Japan

Cover: Foto ©Andreas Hilbeck / pixelio.de

More available books at **www.hansebooks.com**

𝔄 𝔑𝔬𝔳𝔢𝔩.

BY

LADY VIOLET GREVILLE,

AUTHOR OF "ZOE," "KEITH'S WIFE," ETC.

Ye children of man! Whose life is a span.
Protracted with sorrow from day to day,
Naked and featherless, feeble and querulous.
Sickly, calamitous Creatures of Clay."

ARISTOPHANES.

IN THREE VOLUMES.

VOL. III.

LONDON—CHAPMAN AND HALL
. LIMITED.
1885.

WESTMINSTER:
PRINTED BY NICHOLS AND SONS,
25, PARLIAMENT STREET.

CONTENTS.

VOLUME III.

CREATURES OF CLAY.

CHAPTER I.

LUCE was very still. She had seen Granny buried, helped to heap the flowers and the wreaths upon her coffin, knelt in speechless sorrow by the upturned earth, beheld the village turn out with one spontaneous tribute of love and regret, the stalwart young men carrying their heavy burden to the church-yard, an endless procession of mourning folk winding like a long slow worm up the village lane, and she wondered that they could sob and cry and feel. For herself she felt nothing but a cold heavy void. It was so hard, so hard, she kept repeating, that Granny should have been snatched away just as all her hopes were fulfilled— that she should not behold her darling boy triumphant and successful. Hers was all the heart-weariness and sorrow, and she might

not live to see the joy. Luce felt the in-
justice of Life, the cruelty of Fate. To all
of us this feeling of impotent striving and
dumb rage must come in the course of our
lives : to some earlier, to some later, to all
terribly. Whether it be the boy's disappointments or the man's foiled love and ambition,
or the old person's feeble querulousness, to
each and all there comes a moment when we
question Fate, when we try hopelessly to
guess at the enigmas of life, and unravel the
tangled chain of events; when we cry out "If
I had known," or murmur despairingly "It
is no use." And that cry is the worst of all.
It is the open gate to defiance, recklessness,
and negation. Luce's sorrow had stormed
itself out. She was quiet but she was indifferent. Granny's end seemed a useless
sacrifice. Now that she was gone half the
savour of life was gone with her. Luce
scarcely thought of her lover in these days.
He was there, she had given her life to him,
and in due course they would marry, and
Granny's wishes be carried out, but it was
Granny herself that occupied Luce's mind.
Directly after the funeral she had returned
to Highview. Long Leam with Mrs. Vin-

cent as its mistress seemed to her horrible;
Dick, with what she thought unnecessary
courtesy, having intimated to Mrs. Vincent
that she might remain until it suited her to
move. It did not suit Mrs. Vincent at
present; she was really, for once in her life,
ill from vexation and disappointment. To
find that the prize had slipped from her after
all her efforts; that Granny in death, as in
life, true to her affections, left everything in
her will to Dick, and only her savings and a
few personal effects to Vincent, besides the
small fortune to which he was naturally entitled, was a crushing blow. Mrs. Vincent
wandered from room to room wringing her
hands, and lamenting; while the housemaids,
with the alacrity that distinguishes servants
on these occasions, restored things to their
usual places, and rapidly removed all signs
of Granny's presence.

"To think that I should have gained
nothing, nothing!" she moaned to herself,
stopping an instant to scold the maid for
leaving a stray pin upon the carpet. "And
that fool of a husband of mine goes about
the stables just as usual, feeling the horses'
legs and inquiring if they have had exercise;

exercise, psha! when we shan't be able to afford even a carriage for the future."

Mrs. Vincent's opinion of men's wisdom had never been high, but in these days it sank to an unfathomable depth. Even her woman's wit had failed. There was nothing to be done, nothing! With the dead there is no reckoning. Impotent anger and rage filled Mrs Vincent's heart just as it did Luce's, only they were angry with a different object; but it did not alter matters much, the dead are intangible as fate, and as inexorable. Still, there she was for the present, and there she meant to remain as long as possible. Dolly and Eliza laboured at their needlework and drawing as usual, and Vincent went about the stables. Mrs. Vincent tried to imagine that there was nothing changed, but the entire evening's conversation passed in one long querulous lament, Vincent smoking and giving forth an occasional monosyllabic repartee or unintelligible grunt, his wife pouring out a voluble stream of sorrows. Dick was in London busy with deeds and lawyers, Luce had returned home. A cloud of dull repose seemed to have settled upon the Carrol family. Messrs. Cherry and Appleton had announced they did not mean to put in action the warrant against Dick; the unlikelihood of the theft, and the doubtful evidence, were the reasons they gave; in reality they did not wish to quarrel with the new owner of Long Leam, now also become a Member of Parliament. Sir Hilary's death had changed everything; he was no longer there to urge them on, and back up the proceedings. So they wisely argued that the loss was his, and that Lady Fenchurch in her own interest would not press the matter any further.

They were right, as people who speculate on the weaknesses of others usually are. Dick desired nothing better than complete oblivion of the past, and Lady Fenchurch's horror at the sudden shock of her widowhood, fortunately produced a state of nervous ill-health which deprived her of all wish or power to enter upon business matters. But the gossips had a fine feast of it for all that. Dick, always tolerably popular, grew to be a kind of hero, and according to usual custom all the blame was lavished on the woman. Sir Hilary's will revealed the state of his mind, and now that the murder was out Gub-

bins did not scruple to tell all he knew.
Soon it was hinted abroad everywhere that
Sir Hilary had committed suicide, driven to
desperation by his wife's unfaithfulness, and
the partiality she displayed for Dick which
had led her to make him a present of her
pearl-necklace. Dick naturally, as always
happens in such cases, heard nothing of
these reports; and Lady Fenchurch, wrapped
in her mourning and absorbed by her delicate nerves, heard nothing either. So the
public gloated over the scandal, and the scandal grew and grew till it reached Mrs. Vincent's ears. It might have been supposed
that now the concealment of the necklace
could in nowise further Mrs. Vincent's
plans, she would have returned it surrep-
titiously, while keeping herself free from
blame, to its rightful owner; but if she had
lost her money she had at least obtained her
revenge, and Mrs. Vincent was not the
woman to forego that. When through the
gossip of the servants it first became clear to
her that innumerable lies floated about, she
rejoiced greatly. If she suffered it was at
least a kind of meagre satisfaction to think
that others suffered too; that rumour was

busy with a woman's reputation, malignant reports filled the air, and happiness trembled in the balance. Dick, too, might find himself embarrassed by Lady Fenchurch, compromised, and annoyed. If Luce had but one spark of spirit in her she would jilt him, and refuse to play a secondary part. Many things might yet happen, Mrs. Vincent argued; she must wait and see; it should take a great deal to dislodge her from the position she occupied. Perhaps Dick would go abroad, vacate the place if affairs became too vexatious; and then who could better remain and fill the post of trusted manager than Mrs. Vincent? It was to her interest, she reflected, to soothe and humour him; she must make herself necessary, must study his wishes. She began at once by writing to him confidential letters, full of suggestions, pleasant gossip, kindly advice and offers. Dick read the letters with astonishment, remembering the state of open warfare in which they had always lived, and thinking that the loss of Granny must have weakened her head. He speculated for a little, then laid the letters unanswered amid the goodly pile of business communications, bills, circulars, and lawyers' epistles with which he was surrounded. Mrs. Vincent meanwhile burrowed like a mole in the tortuous underground passages she was labouring to excavate; discovered the butler drank the sherry, and wrote to Dick to ask if she should dismiss him in the latter's interests, then knocked off one of the under-gardeners, declaring that it was no use keeping seven men to do the work of six. The poor fellow, morose and disheartened, returned to his wife, just risen from her bed with a new-born baby in her arms, while three other small children toddled about and clutched at her skirts, and talked of applying to the parish. But Mrs. Vincent believed she had done a good deed and saved the new owner of Long Leam fourteen shillings a week, which in these necessitous times is no trifle. She sent the chintzes to be washed, and put all Granny's books away in a cupboard; " nasty freethinking works they were too," she remarked by the way to the old housemaid.

The latter wondered and murmured that " Missus had always been a God-fearing lady."

" No doubt, Ann, no doubt," accentuated

Mrs. Vincent, "but that was in spite of reading those bad books; she would have been better without them, and you know the Lord's Prayer says 'Lead us not into temptation'—bad books are a great temptation. I hope you will never read them, Ann."

"Lor' bless you, mum," said old Ann with a laugh," I'm no scholard, though my niece, the third housemaid, is; she can read beautiful, print and handwriting and all."

"There's the danger, Ann, young people are so easily puffed up; tell her to mind, and to come to me for her books."

Mrs. Vincent was feeling better; it did her good, and braced her up to give advice, and she flicked away with the duster she carried right merrily.

"Yes, Ann," continued Mrs. Vincent; "things have been happy-go-lucky here too long. You all want brushing up; poor old Mrs. Carrol was past her work; latterly she had grown doting; she had a habit of believing everybody; and you know, Ann, that leads to everybody cheating you."

"Indeed, 'mum," said Ann, inserting her gaunt body between an ebony cabinet and

the wall, in order to pursue cleaning oper-
ations more commodiously.

"Yes, Ann. Of course it is quite right
that you should respect your late mistress;
she left you a nice little legacy to buy mourning with, and all that, but abuses which were
very well in the old days must be done away
with now. For instance, that unlimited
beer. Now you don't tell me it is necessary
for a woman to have five meals a day, and
beer and cheese at eleven o'clock. It's
positively disgusting. You don't take luncheon, I hope?"

She turned suddenly, and found the unfortunate Ann, who, wiping her mouth with
her apron, thought sorrowfully of the lun-
cheon-hour, which was 'already past and
gone.

"Well, mum, one feels a little dry if one
has been up since six o'clock, always dust-
ing and muddling about in the dirt."

"Dry, indeed! A respectable woman
should not give way to the sins of the flesh.
I never take luncheon."

', No, mum; but ladies is different."

"I should hope they were, indeed! But,
if I am spared here, please God, I see before

me a sphere of endless usefulness. I shall effect a revolution."

"I am sure you will, mum." And Ann, reflecting that with her little savings she could live comfortably in a cottage of her own, determined at once to give warning.

Thus admonishing, Mrs. Vincent almost felt happy. She had the rare faculty of believing in herself; she never doubted her own intentions nor distrusted her own capacity; if there was anything to be done she could do it, and do it better than any one else. And this sense of perfect self-satisfaction stood her in good stead in the ordinary difficulties of life.

She felt herself born to rule, and resented it as a grievance if she were forced to obey. The rude coarseness of her husband and the meek submission of her well-trained daughters nourished this belief, for who could fail to be superior to a lout who drank brandy-and-water, and preferred the company of stable-men; or to girls who had seen and known nothing of the world, and merely answered "Yes, mamma," to all observations. Mrs. Vincent laboured under the disadvantage of living only with people who were

manifestly her inferiors, or with those who
for their own ends pretended to be so. As
lady patroness at bazaars, as secretary of the
Young Women's Aid Society, or dispenser of
clothing-clubs, her energy and stubbornness
were appreciated and required; and she was
so accustomed to observe her friends bow
down to her decisions and refrain from
questioning her judgment, that she ceased
to think of herself as fallible. The consciousness of high rectitude produced a kind of
warp in her conscience which enabled her to
commit with impunity, actions which in
others she would have styled reprehensible,
if not absolutely criminal. If it be therefore
asked how Mrs. Vincent contrived to com-
bine piety with unscrupulousness, the answer
is that her piety was so compounded as to
cover a multitude of sins with a conveniently
thin mantle of propriety. Occasionally, perhaps, pricks of conscience made themselves
felt, rapidly however subdued by the reflection that her liver must be out of order, otherwise things would appear as usual in a
pleasing and meritorious light. Uncle Vincent
was not so happy as his wife. He reproached
himself acutely for the part he had taken in

the election, saying bitterly that if he had known which way the wind blew, he would have stuck to the ship in spite of everything. Now, of course, he had alienated his nephew for ever. It was not likely he would ever befriend him again, buy horses of him, or take his opinion about a bet. It was deuced unfortunate, certainly, but then no power on earth could foresee that Granny would die without altering her will, that Dick would succeed in getting into Parliament, and that Sir Hilary would be such a madman as to cut his own throat, (for the belief in suicide was now generally diffused.) Vincent meditated sorrowfully, he was verging on middle age, and he had no prospects; his sons were growing up, and his own appetite for racing and horse-flesh remained undiminished; his weight had increased too, and his purse grown lighter, his indulgent mother was dead, and his wife though admirable could scarcely be called indulgent. In tobacco alone he found a solace; it was a cheap and a satisfactory luxury—it eased the mind, and dulled the brain; and so long as a man could look at the future through a cloud of smoke, he was not so very much to be pitied. So he withdrew himself more and more from female society, and was never to be seen without a pipe in his mouth. That, at least at present, he comforted himself, was a habit and a privilege reserved for the stronger sex, and one of which it would require some years exercise of the female franchise to deprive the lords of the creation.

CHAPTER II.

MATTERS at Highview Castle were similarly in confusion. At first a general sense of triumph, neatly tempered by decorous mourning for Mrs. Carrol, animated every-one. Now, however, that the first sense of jubilation had worn off, various causes combined to produce a reaction. First and fore-most, Mr. Highview was not quite satisfied about the affair of the necklace. While the election lasted, excitement and business caused him to regard Dick's conduct in a more favourable light, but now Mr. Highview felt strongly that his going off to London, and apparent absorption in the affairs of his property, showed a want of respect and proper regard for his future uncle's feelings. Mr. Highview himself was blessed with an inconvenient delicacy, which made him careful not to offend, but which, *per contra*, inclined him to exact more from his neighbours. This sensitive, impressionable nature was shared by his daughter, and formed one of the reasons of her dislike to general society. Lady Eleanor, on her part, in her drives and visits, had heard the story of the supposed suicide, considerably garbled and added to, and began to fear that a man so hampered, morally and socially, could scarcely prove a desirable husband. Not that the moral responsibilities affected her deeply, but the social difficulties were of course not easily to be got over. Lady Fenchurch's position might prove a difficulty, Dick foolishly think himself bound to marry, now he had compromised her; and, even if he declined, she might hamper him with claims and petulances sufficient to make his life a burden. Lady Eleanor was not disturbed by the contemplation of Dick's unhappiness, but her pride revolted at the idea of Luce coming off second best, and of her young niece's domestic affairs being the talk of the county. One may have corns, but so long as nobody else perceives, by one's limping gait that the shoe pinches, little irrevocable harm is done. Such was

Lady Eleanor's view of life, she regarded from the outside and based it solely on superficial appearances. No one had less patience than Lady Eleanor with maudlin sentimentalities, or the feeble self-torturings of morbid women; she had a grand constitution and splendid health, and recognised no evils but a doubtful social position. Maud, as usual her confidant in the matter, cordially agreed, remarking that Lady Eleanor was always right.

"Ah, my dear!" placidly observed the elder lady, turning her hand round to note the brilliant flashing of the gems upon her white fingers, "if everyone had your common sense, girls and boys would not be so difficult to manage; you are remarkably prudent and far-seeing for your age; but Luce, on the contrary, is quite a child, and so romantic."

Maud concurred, deploring unprofitable romance.

"After all," continued Lady Eleanor, lounging luxuriously among the cushions of her boudoir, "a trip abroad, a short absence, will assist the forgetfulness of the world. Society asks no better than to condone the follies of the rich, and Dick will be rich now. Perhaps a honeymoon tour will do all that is necessary, and Luce is so plain that to find an eligible husband might be difficult. You, of course, Maud, handsome as you are, have had even less chance." Lady Eleanor never spared friends more than enemies. "Men don't care to saddle themselves with pauper relations."

"I don't think my husband will be troubled by relations," said Maud, tossing her head.

"Quite right, my dear, sensible as usual; an impecunious mother-in-law always in want of a dinner and borrowing a shilling to pay her cabs is the very thing a man dreads."

"He need not dread it in my case."

"But then you see they do not know. I am sure young Mr. Sterney for instance could not face such a prospect."

"No; he spends too much on burlesque actresses to have anything to spare for his mother-in-law."

"Exactly so; but to return to Luce. Of course it is my earnest desire to get the child provided for. I have done my duty

by her hitherto, but I shall not consider I
have been a real mother to her till I see her
well settled. If I was quite sure about
Dick ——"

"Can you not speak to him, ask him to
be honest and straightforward?"

"Men are never honest to one woman
about another."

"That is a difficulty."

"Then there is the woman. It is impossible to foresee how Lady Fenchurch will
behave."

"She has ordered her mourning. I saw it
at Miss Shear's in West Thorpe, beautiful
crape, and quite a new style of trimming.
You know how hideous and heavy crape
usually is, now this was positively becoming."

"That is a very bad sign. A widow who
thinks of what is becoming does not mean to
mourn long."

"Dr. Pilule is always with her they say."

"He is a young man: this is worse and
worse."

"I suppose Dick knows his own affairs
best; he is engaged to Luce."

"Yes, and that is my greatest comfort.

He understands what is due to our family and position—he never would dare to play fast and loose with Mr. Highview's daughter."

"I suppose not," said Maud, bitterly, reflecting that men would be troubled by no such scruples in her own case.

"Certainly not. And Luce has been so well brought up that she will do whatever she is told."

Luce herself made her appearance at that instant, and the conversation was presently pitched in another key, but Luce had heard enough to cause her to understand that in some way her fate was involved. The same evening, breaking through the indifference she had displayed since Granny's death, she followed Maud into the cosy chintz room, whose luxuries had not yet lost their charm for that young lady, " Maud ! dear ——" she hesitated.

" Well, what is it ? help me off with this dress, please, what a bore things are that fasten behind. I notice you always wear full bodies and bands; quite right, they are not half the trouble."

"Oh! I have no figure. I don't care a bit about the fit of a dress as you do."

"You should care more, Luce." Maud fixed her bright mocking eyes on her friend's face. "If you don't take care, you'll be made a catspaw of ——"

"Maud, you have heard something; what is it?"

"Have you guessed nothing, you innocent baby?"

Maud sat down in front of her glass and proceeded to uncoil her beautiful hair, touching it lovingly and delicately, with the reverence due from a beautiful woman to one of her chief weapons of fascination. Luce watched her silently; as an artist she was keenly alive to the subtle charm of beauty.

"And so you have guessed nothing, you poor dear! How long is it since you have heard from Dick?"

"Dick! He does not write often."

"So I should think. And have you talked of the wedding day——?"

"Oh, Maud, I am in no hurry; poor Granny is only just dead, remember." Luce dropped into a chair, and laid her hands in her lap.

"Granny was an old woman and you and Dick are young; you cannot mourn for ever, it is scarcely flattering to your intended."

"He has said nothing yet."

"Has it never occurred to you that he might have reasons for not hurrying on his marriage? Usually, a lover is impatient for the woman to name the day."

"A lover, yes." Luce thought to herself that where the love was on one side only, things might be different.

"He *is* your lover, I suppose, as you are engaged to him, and you have always talked so much about not marrying for anything but love."

"Yes," echoed Luce, in a faint voice.

"Very well then; if I were you I should not be satisfied to have his name coupled with that of another woman ——"

"Another woman!" The voice though faint was no longer listless.

"Another woman, an old love, Lady Fenchurch."

"Who couples their names? What do you mean? It is all a lie." Luce's eyes flashed, as quiet orbs can, when their owners are strongly excited.

"If you were not so absorbed in your own thoughts you would hear what is said around you and know *this* is not a lie."

"Not a lie?"

"You echo like a parrot. Don't you want to know what is said about you and Dick?"

"Yes."

"With all your philosophy you're as sensitive to the opinions of others as any-one I know."

"Go on, please," said Luce, with a gasp, steeling herself to endure a moral surgical operation.

"So I will when I have arranged my thoughts. Did you ever hear the particulars of Sir Hilary Fenchurch's death?"

"Of course I heard he was dead—of a fit, I think – but I had never seen him, you know."

"And therefore, though a good Christian, you could only pay him complimentary mourning, but yet his death affects you personally. Do you know how he died?"

"No."

"He committed suicide." Maud leant forward and darted out these words with the tragic precision of an accomplished actress.

She did not miss her point. Luce started back.

"He, suicide! Why?"

"Because he found out something about his wife and Dick that did not please him—and because—can't you guess?"

"Lady Fenchurch!" Luce clasped her hands together nervously, trying to clear her brain sufficiently to comprehend the gist of the matter. "Lady Fenchurch is nothing to Dick—it is all a mistake."

"A mistake then that is likely to have remarkably disagreeable consequences," observed Maud, plaiting up her hair. "When a woman's husband commits suicide on account of her love affairs, especially if he disinherits her in his will, it is not likely to improve her position in the world."

"Do people say this?" asked Luce, her eyes wide open in a stare of puzzled terror.

"They say it, and also that she gave Dick her necklace to pay his debts—it was never found, you remember; and now you know as much as I do about the matter." Maud turned to her looking-glass and stuck her heavy plait up with hair-pins. There was silence for a few moments. Luce breathed painfully but she did not speak. Maud was obliged to look over her shoulder to note the effect of her communication.

"How silent you are—don't you care? I must say Dick has not treated you well; however, I suppose he would hardly tell you all this, and he trusted that you would never find it out. Poor child, did it mind? Believe me, there are as good fish in the sea as ever came out of it."

"I suppose you meant kindly in telling me this," Luce said, as she rose slowly, knotting her hands while she spoke, "but I wish—I wish I were still in ignorance."

"Of course you do; but really, Luce, it is better sometimes to look things in the face. Wilful ignorance is the act of a fool."

"You have often called me a fool. I suppose everyone who trusts and believes in a fellow-creature is a fool?"

"Don't become cynical, Luce, it is bad taste now—everyone talks of universal brotherhood--pray don't go away in this abrupt manner." Luce made a movement towards the door. "You look so pale, and you won't sleep, and only fret yourself to death. Do stay, and let us talk it over."

"I cannot talk, I feel choked."

"You are dreadfully sensitive," said
Maud, looking complacently at her own
fair face in the glass; "there is not a bit of
use in being too good for this world."

"The world is too good for me," said
Luce, escaping as she uttered this paradox.
Maud shrugged her shoulders. She had
experienced already so many slips between
the cup and the lip that she grew to regard
them as part of the world's economy, and
reflected that, after all, she was none the
worse—if one marriage fell through, it was
easy to look about for another. As long as
youth and beauty endured there was no
ground for despondency; but then Luce, she
supposed, really cared. What a silly a girl
must be, *really* to care. Maud, smiling at
her friend's infatuation, placed her candle
by her bedside and laid a new railway novel
close to it, with which she purposed to read
herself to sleep; then she fell upon her knees
and said her prayers. The habit taught her
and persevered in from childhood, had
become second nature. The petitions she
presented were generally mechanical, sometimes almost pagan in their outspokenness,

yet it was one of the few practices she clung
to superstitiously. She could never tell; she
might be seized with illness, a fire might
break out, it was better to say one's prayers,
and have some kind of claim on the protec-
tion of the Deity. After that, an exciting
novel to lull one to sleep offered an agreeable variety.

Luce, shut up in her small bedchamber,
which Lady Eleanor considered sufficiently
furnished with the barest and simplest of
necessaries, knelt down to no evening
prayers with the calm indifference of Maud.
She locked the door, placed the candle on
the dressing-table, and began to walk up
and down, up and down, restlessly. The
wild animal which is in each of us was let
loose; she could not rest, she could not sit,
she wanted movement; she had mourned so
deeply and vicariously for Granny, her
thoughts had been lately raised so much to
Heaven and the joys and mystery of eternity,
that it caused her a shock and a wrench to
fix them suddenly on more mundane objects,
to decide what was truth in the world's
verdict, and reflect on the duties owing to
society. Society, the fetish to which her

young life had always been sacrificed; the
insatiable monster that had swallowed up all
her youthful impulses, and turned her most
innocent joys to gall. In her marriage at
least, she had hoped to escape from the bond-
age of society; she was taking the man she
loved, without afterthought of rank or
fortune; with him she meant to lead a true,
a natural, a human life, there were to be no
clouds between them, no shadow of an un-
truth. He had told her plainly about his
former love, he had done nothing underhand
towards that love, all had seemed simple and
straightforward and clear, but now—Luce
pressed her hands to her head, the throbbing
veins seemed as though they would burst.
Suicide was a crime. Luce, reared in
Christian habits of thought, could not persuade herself that men had the right to throw
away the precious gift of life whenever they
were weary and sick at heart; it was cowardly,
she felt, to desert a post of danger—nothing
could palliate or excuse the crime. And to
this, Dick and the wretched man's wife were
partners. They had driven Sir Hilary to
the despair that prompted the deed—they
were partners in guilt. The world had

already visited some of the consequences upon the woman; her reputation was assailed. Defenceless, she could only go to destruction; Dick must not leave her now. Formerly it had appeared a duty for him to forget her, and to marry another woman, it seemed like closing the forbidden book, and turning strenuously away to a higher and a mightier right; now the poor sinning creature had a claim to the man's compassion, his service, and his love. Luce shuddered. The shadow of the cross had fallen on her life, the great mystery of sacrifice and suffering was revealed to her. Just because she was the stronger— because, in the power of her love, she could soar above the petty interests and scruples of ordinary folk—for that very reason it was her duty to take the initiative, to plunge the dagger into her own heart, and draw it out again smiling. She thrust open the window, for a breath of air. The sky was dark with deepest blue, and pierced with stars, which flickered and twinkled in innumerable clusters. They seemed to befriend her, to encourage her in the vastness which made her feel only one small trembling unit in the throbbing universe. Her one little ife was

so short, her one sacrifice so infinitesimal,
while the mighty right was eternal and
immutable. Gradually her heart ceased to
beat so violently, a sense of cold calmed the
fever in her veins. The trees rustled faintly
in the chill night air. She waited till the
crowing of a distant cock, and the gradual
sotto-voce tuning of the birds awaking from
their nests, warned her it was morning.
Then she slowly shut the window and withdrew into the room, which now felt damp
and chilly. She undressed quickly, and,
shivering, flung herself into bed. Everything bright and beautiful was slipping from
her; she welcomed the mere sense of fatigue
and exhaustion, that lulled her nerves, and
numbed the aching pain that gripped her
in its powerful grasp.

CHAPTER III.

Luce was not one to let the grass grow under her feet; she shrank and quivered keenly under the blow that struck her; but the resolve formed in her midnight hour of communion beneath the friendly stars, never for an instant deserted her. She knew that she had renounced happiness, but when she saw the straight path of duty stretching out clearly before her, she felt calmer and quieter. There is that advantage to be gained in acting rather on principle than on impulse, that once a decision is formed, a sense of peace and directness immediately becomes its accompaniment. Luce appeared at breakfast the next morning calm and unruffled; and Maud, who looked up quickly at her entrance, expecting to see some traces of the night's struggle, noticed nothing at all remarkable in her appearance, but an almost imperceptible quiver of the eyelids. Lady Eleanor's toilet, which was of an elaborate description, requiring both time and attention on the part of a first-rate French maid, never permitted her to appear much before noon. If, therefore, any one of the family desired to speak to her, it was necessary to ask for entrance to her bed-room. Luce, as soon as the family meal was over, knocked at her door. Lady Eleanor thought she had come about some arrangements for a prospective dinner-party, and admitted her at once.

" Will you write the invitations, Luce ? Here are some cards." Luce submitted, and, taking a seat at the writing-table, obediently indited notes and directed envelopes. When she had finished and Lady Eleanor leant back reflectively in her arm-chair trying to remember if any one had been inadvertently forgotten, she said quietly, holding her pen still wet with ink before her,

"Aunt, do you object to my asking Dick here to spend the day ? I have some matters to talk over, and writing is difficult."

Lady Eleanor started. Could the child have overheard her conversation ? Was she anxious to press on the marriage so as to leave no loophole of escape to her future husband? On second thoughts, she decided that Luce had not sufficient guile in her composition to render such scheming likely.

"You wish to see Dick?" she answered after a pause which made Luce look up nervously.

"Yes, aunt, I have scarcely seen him since our engagement and so many things have happened; there is no objection surely."

"No certainly, no objection." Lady Eleanor passed her thin cambric handkerchief across her mouth. "But Dick is in London. I fancy he is detained by business."

"It is only a few hours' journey from town, Dick thinks nothing of travelling."

"Well, it is for him to decide; do you wish me to write and invite him?"

"If you do not mind, I will write myself."

"Certainly." Lady Eleanor was puzzled. Luce did not generally act with decision, in fact the formal accusation brought against her was of being always in the clouds. "I suppose you wish to speak to him about the wedding-day, it is rather strange that he should not already have mentioned it."

"No, no, he is in deep mourning and we are in no hurry; it is better that we should learn to know each other."

This was not at all what Lady Eleanor desired. She had a horror of long engagements.

"I hope to goodness, my dear, your engagement will not drag on indefinitely. Nothing is so injurious both to the temper and the prospects of a young person."

"I don't think you need fear. It will not drag on interminably," said Luce with a strange smile.

"Very well then, you can write to Dick."

Luce availed herself of the desired permission, but forbore to announce the fact to Maud, who consumed herself in helpless wonder as to the course events were taking.

Dick answered Luce's letter in the affirmative, and a few day later she made her way down the approach, to meet him on his arrival from the station. The dog-cart had been sent for him, and very soon she espied

him driving it himself, and looking particularly bright and and happy. Luce was nervous and miserable. There is something so
cruel in being the bearer of bad news, to one
who advances unconsciously to his fate with a
smile on his lips and perfect trust in his
heart. For an instant Luce regretted that
she had ever invited him; she could have
written, it would have been easier, and then
she need not have seen his smiling happy
face unclouded by a care before her, while
she uttered the fateful words. No, that was a
cowardly thought after all; she had no reason
to suppose he would care; did he not tell her
he only married to please his grandmother?
Possibly he would thank Luce for what she
was going to say. She braced herself to
smile at him and say good morning. He
pulled up immediately, threw the reins to
the groom, and jumped out. In another
instant he was walking beside her, away
from the house towards the shrubbery.

"It was very jolly of you to send for me,
Luce," he said lightly, breaking off a bit of
laurustinus and sticking it in his button hole.
"I shouldn't have thought of coming if you
had not written, for I don't believe Lady

Eleanor appreciates my company particularly."

"Oh yes, Dick, she has spoken so kindly of you lately."

"I find everyone much kinder since I have succeeded to Long Leam," he said with a laugh. "After all, the world is a good place to live in, provided one has plenty of money."

"Dick!"

"Don't preach, Luce. I'm going to be awfully steady, pay all my debts, (that tailor of mine, who used always to dun me, now does nothing but beg me for custom and offer me credit,) it's a real joke, I can tell you, and then I'm going to keep up the old place just as Granny liked, and you can look upon the fine house she was so proud of, as your own property. I think she would be pleased if she knew, don't you, Luce?"

"I wonder if she does know. Don't you think love must be subtle enough to pierce through space, and that even in heaven she must feel how much we love her, and how we miss her? Dick, she was so good to me, no human being ever was so good to me."

"She was an old dear," responded Dick, flogging with his light cane at the tall grasses by the shrubbery walk. "I'm extremely grateful to her. I don't know how I could have gone on much longer, I was horribly pressed for money."

Luce put her hand to her heart. This speech more than corroborated all she had been told. The debts, the gift of the necklace, Lady Fenchurch's acceptable help.

"You will not want it so much now," she said quietly.

"Oh, no! I shall take care. It is a great nuisance being in debt, but what is a fellow to do if he has not got the means?"

"I suppose one ought to deny oneself the luxuries one cannot afford?"

"You speak like a girl. What is the use of being a young man with prospects if one is to live like an ascetic old monk? However, thank goodness, that is all past and over now, and I shall be a model for the future—when we are married!" He turned and kissed her cheek impulsively.

"Oh, Dick!"

"Nonsense! don't play the little prude; we shall be married soon now, I supppose?"

He drew her hand within his arm, and patted it kindly. His cordiality, his *insouciance*, his evident happiness, made Luce's task harder. Her hopes died away, and her courage receded. After all, if he were satisfied, and glad to have her, and strained after no desires or discontented longings, why should she stir up muddy depths in the brightly springing fountain of his life? With a desperate determination she said,

"Dick, was not that dreadful about Sir Hilary?"

"Dreadful, dear, but it was lucky for me, too."

"Lucky?"

"Well, you know, that beastly affair about the necklace was still hanging over me, and now, of course, it is at an end."

"And you are glad?"

"Naturally."

"Oh! how I wish the thief could be found!"

"So do I." But Dick's voice was far less enthusiastic than that of Luce.

Her fears deepened. Surely no one who was perfectly innocent could talk so calmly. She had not yet quite comprehended Dick's nature, which, easily diverted from serious thought, attached no importance to facts of which the consequences were remote. As long as he saw himself threatened with so positive an evil as a jail, he suffered acutely, but the instant the immediate danger was removed he could talk with equanimity, or even sneer at intangible and unlikely difficulties. Luce liked to grapple firmly with a danger or an annoyance, to face it bravely, and note all its bearings; he preferred to evade, to procrastinate, to forget. The one temperament is essentially lymphatic, and of the soap-bubble kind, and results in a smooth gentlemanly egoism, which carries its owner agreeably over the shallows and rapids down the stream of life, until it meets with some overwhelming crashing torrent, in which it utterly collapses. The other temperament, nervous and excitable, spares no pains, and intensifies each trouble as it comes, but in the long run the dangers are surmounted, the rocks avoided, and the slender bark sails quietly out into the calm ocean. Luce wondered at Dick's unconcern, and attached far graver importance to it than it deserved.

"Dick," she continued, timidly, twisting a bit of grass between her fingers. "Dick, what will become of Lady Fenchurch?"

"Lady Fenchurch? By Jove, how should *I* know what becomes of pretty women when they are widows? I suppose she is rich, and she is young and independent, she will probably travel at first, and eventually marry."

"But—her first love?"

"Her first love? Oh! you mean her fancy for me. I am sure I don't know if it was her first love, I should think that very unlikely. Well, I suppose she has got over it now; we had enough annoyance about it. I don't think it was all roses for her with that old curmudgeon of a husband, and at any rate I am going to be married now."

"We are not married yet."

"Not yet; but I don't see why we should lose any time about it. I am my own master, and Mrs. Vincent must turn out whenever I choose."

There was a pleasant conviction of power and freedom about Dick as he said these words. Not so very long ago Mrs. Vincent ruled supreme, and had the power to expel him from the house of which he was now the fortunate owner. The tables were certainly turned upon her in a most satisfactory fashion. Dick raised his head and threw back his shoulders with a consciously satisfied movement.

"But, Dick, there are others to be considered," said the gentle tremulous voice at his side.

"Of course I shall consider you." Her hand had dropped from his arm, and the pale earnest face was turned away from him.

"I do not mean myself, I mean Lady Fenchurch."

Dick gave a long whistle.

"By Jove! I don't think I need consider her, I thought we settled all that long ago."

"But remember this dreadful story about the suicide, the poor thing is penniless and her reputation damaged."

The pale face was turned towards him now and glowed with passionate pleading.

"What do you mean? Really, Luce, excuse me, but I do not think this is at all your business."

"Yes, Dick it *is* my business; I should never feel happy if I were the means of making another woman wretched. She loved you and you loved her once, and she has lost a great—great deal for you—what a woman prizes most in the world, her good name, and I—how have I deserved to be so happy ? "

" Because you are a first-rate good sterling little woman," said her lover warmly, clutching at the hand she tried to withdraw from him, and getting it again into his possession. The pressure of his fingers thrilled through her body; she was longing to love him ; it seemed very hard, of her own accord to give him up.

" Oh, Dick, don't praise me; indeed, indeed, I'm not good or strong or wise, but I want you to be all that."

" So I shall, some day. I am sure you'll live to be proud of me; you shall have everything you like, horses and dogs, and yards of flannel for the poor people, and the parson to dinner whenever you please."

" No, no, don't tempt me, do try and understand, you can't build a house on a sandy foundation; your whole life mustn't be founded on a wrong; you must be strong and noble, strong for me and yourself."

"I can't be strong without you. Now what do you want me to do?"

"Not to forsake the poor woman whose love for you has caused her so much suffering."

"How?"

"I mean you must marry her and not me."

Luce's head drooped. Her serious eyes no longer sought his to persuade and strengthen.

"You are mad," he let her hand go angrily, "you must be mad."

"No, Dick, I have thought seriously and deeply, you owe her this reparation."

"Stuff!"

"Dick do, do let us try to act rightly."

"Act like lunatics, you mean," he said, biting at his moustache, "what would everyone say? Besides, I don't care to marry her now, when she has been talked about."

"Oh Dick, is that kind and manly? Her faults are yours, her mistakes are yours, her troubles were caused by you; she is free, she is alone and defenceless, to whom can she look for comfort but to you?"

"This is not fair, Luce, you have no right

to make such an appeal to me. I understood you pretended to care for me?"

"So I do, I care more than ever I did." A big tear rose to her eyes, but she dashed it away with her hand, "it is because I care I say these things."

"I must say it is a droll kind of affection," he answered, dryly, "that hands a man over to some other woman, a woman too who has played fast and loose with him——"

"Still she loved you."

"I think she loved herself better."

"It is the privilege of a man to protect a woman."

"Certainly, but he is not bound to protect all women."

Luce ceased speaking. She had exhausted her powers of argument and persuasion. Naturally inclined to be silent, it had cost her no slight effort to say all she did. She felt sick and weary, and very hopeless. The path, along which they were walking, would at any other moment have delighted her with its singular beauty. They were in a species of wild shrubbery allowed to grow in luxurious negligence and indulge the full exuberance of nature. Sturdy rhododendron bushes extended in glossy symmetrical mounds as far as the gravel. Between them, among ferns and grasses, a blue carpet of hyacinths spread away into the distance; at her feet heavy-headed daffodils swayed and nodded gently; laburnum and lilac trees, their brown branches tipped with little green points, overarched her head, and small drops of glistening dew fell as she brushed against the overhanging boughs; or touched the blades of wet grass with her skirts. Luce felt the beauty of the scene as one feels some person tapping outside a glass window that one can see without hearing any noise; it was all beautiful, she knew it was beautiful—the budding spring, the early flowers with their bright colours, and the dewiness, and freshness, and sweetness, and yet it did not touch her. Dick walked on, angrily swishing his cane at the innocent daffodils, and she followed, breathlessly, feeling sorry for the poor pretty things.

"And so you wish to be quit of me? I understand; perhaps I am not rich enough, or you believe all the nonsense you have heard, or you care for some one else."

"No, no," she panted.

"If I thought—Luce I shall never forgive you, never, never. I was a fool; I fancied that you cared for me, really for me, not for my position, or my name, or—and you're just like the others, you only think of your-self, you only consider your own happiness."

"Oh, Dick, indeed ——"

"Don't explain anything, I don't want to hear, I will marry Lady Fenchurch if you wish it. I daresay she will be pleasant and amiable enough: she will have her own way in everything, but I shall never trust a woman again, never, never!"

He stopped breathless with anger.

"Dick," she began soothingly, "please don't imagine I am thinking of myself. I— oh, you know Dick what I feel."

"How can I tell what a girl feels? Ca-pricious, foolish, heartless creature."

"But don't you see that our duty, yours and mine, is to Lady Fenchurch?"

"I don't see it a bit, I don't acknowledge any duty, I refuse to acknowledge anything but your wishes and our love."

"Our love! Did not you always tell me you had only loved Lady Fenchurch; that I"—she pressed her hands against her bosom, and the big tears rained down—"was only to be a kind of companion, a sister, to please Granny?"

"Oh well," he said in a kinder tone, "I daresay I did not mean all I said; I was very sore about Lady Fenchurch then, but I see things more quietly now; come, Luce, don't be a little fool, I always thought you *such* a sensible girl; say you will marry me, and let us forget all this nonsense."

Luce shook her head, the sobs were coming thick and fast, in another moment she would not be able to control them.

"What—you won't? Oh yes, try to be a good little girl."

Luce made an effort; what must he think of her, offering to give him up, and crying like a baby as she did so? Where was her philosophy, her firm resolve, her determined self-denial?

"Dick, we had better not discuss the matter any more. My mind is made up."

"And you won't marry me—you refuse—calmly intend to jilt me—is that your last word?"

"I think you ought to give me up and ask Lady Fenchurch to marry you."

"And of course she will," he said bitterly.

" Here's a nice state of things—to be saddled with a woman you don't want and lose the woman you do. I declare I'm the most unlucky fellow in the world."

" Dick, I am so sorry," she said, stealing her hand into his with the confidence of a child.

" And it's your fault if I'm unhappy," he said, dropping her hand with an angry jerk, " all your fault; you said you would take me in hand, that you cared for me; and it was all going right, I felt so happy and so good as I came down here, thinking of you and all we were going to do—by Jove, I hadn't felt so good since I was a boy in knicker-bockers and saved up my money to buy toffee, and now you've smashed up the whole thing; if I go to the devil it's all your fault."

Luce sighed. He heard the sigh and proceeded more glibly.

" But there, when women want to annoy one they can do it, trust them for that, first Lady Fenchurch and then you. Do you really mean all you have just said, or were you only trying me ? "

" I mean it."

" Then good-bye, there is no use in wasting any more words about it," he pulled out his watch, and looked at it; " I can just walk across the fields, and catch the next train back to town, while you explain the cause of my non-appearance to Lady Eleanor."

" Surely, Dick, you will not go like this, Mr. Highview expected you."

" And I expected a very different welcome also, but you see I was mistaken, and he will have to bear his disappointment as best he can. Good-bye." He spoke roughly and turned to go, then seeing Luce's imploring look he stopped and said, " Luce, on my solemn word of honour I'm sorry to leave you, shake hands with me and wish me luck. I've a kind of queer feeling that you can bring it if you choose."

Luce put out her hand and looked at him with all the yearning love of her heart visible in her clear eyes; he didnot stay to look, but squeezed the hand she gave him passionately, then without another word he left her, standing alone and comfortless in the dewy path.

CHAPTER IV.

THE hardest part of Luce's task was not finished with that interview in the shrubbery. In moments of great mental tension there is a power that raises us above the level of ordinary emotion, the Lethe of excitement dulls the pain and renders us impervious to the suffering we are enduring. But when the friendly Lethe leaves us, when we see the full extent of the sacrifice, behold our life stripped of the love we willingly surrendered, are pricked by sneers or irritated by well-meaning comfort and advice, then indeed we realise the meaning of our loss. The sweet spring day, the brilliant sunshine growing warmer as the hours proceeded, the birds' airy flight skimming low over the smooth shaven lawns, the merry capers and abrupt pauses of the little rabbits darting in and out, were loathsome to poor Luce; never had the way home seemed so long, never had her steps lagged so wearily. It all had to be faced; the surprised looks of the men-servants gathered to relieve Dick of his wraps and luggage as she entered alone, the kindly questioning of Mr. Highview in the library where the door stood open so that she could not pass unobserved, Lady Eleanor's astonishment, her regret for the elaborate toilet she had unnecessarily made, mingled with anger for her niece's folly, Maud's evident amusement and undisguised contempt. Luce braved it all with a quiet unconcern that she herself wondered at. Though her heart felt fit to break and she was desperately longing to throw herself on some friendly bosom and weep out her sorrows, she found strength to answer Lady Eleanor's torrent of inquiries, and to hold her own in the vindictive cross-examination.

"And he seemed pleased to see you and was very kind?" said Lady Eleanor in her iciest satirical voice.

"Yes certainly, he was very kind."

"And you actually broke off your engagement?"

"We agreed that it was best so." Here Luce took her stand, and to all efforts to break through the defences of love, shame, and vanity only answered, "It was best so."

"And do you know, Miss, what it means to be a jilted girl?" asked Lady Eleanor, magnificent in her rising wrath.

"I can guess."

"No one will believe for a moment that *you* broke it off; girls never do those things; they will say he was tired of you, that you were deformed, or had bad health, or a bad temper."

"I cannot help it."

"Ungrateful minx!" and Lady Eleanor sailed from the room to overwhelm her husband with reproaches and lamentations.

Kind Mr. Highview was sorely distressed. He was tolerably ignorant of girls' natures, and could not tell how much they meant of what they said, but he felt pretty certain that Luce loved Dick, and that it caused her a pang to give him up. Personally he saw no necessity for her sacrificing herself to an abstract sense of duty, especially for a woman who had been *talked about*. Mr. Highview had all a respectable man's

horror of a lady's tarnished reputation, but
he could not refrain from according Luce,
however grudgingly, a meed of respectful
admiration.   He knew his wife's persistency
and her love of rule too well not to anticipate with dread on Luce's behalf the annoyances her conduct must necessarily entail.
Like a man too, he endeavoured to explain
away matters, to expostulate, and to soothe,
and succeeded neither in allaying Lady
Eleanor's wrath nor in materially assisting
Luce.   Such are the excellent but feeble
natures that endeavour to stem revolutions
with partial concessions, or throw themselves
into the breach of parties with a pleasant
observation or a text from the Bible.   In an
instant their frail interposition is brushed
aside like the advances of an impertinent
fly, and their advice promptly disregarded.

" But, my dear," poor Mr. Highview suggested, " you see it may be only a little misunderstanding, a lover's quarrel.   I am sure
we had our lover's quarrels, once upon a
time, too."

" I am sure *we* never had lover's quarrels
indeed, I never was a fool if you were Mr.

Highview, and I tell you Luce has broken her engagement, turned young Carrol off, given him his liberty."

" He will return to her."

" Will he ? I doubt it. Freedom is too pleasant to a gay and rich young man for him to give it up lightly."

" Well, at least it is better not to marry in haste and repent at leisure."

" I am sure if women did not marry in haste they would never marry at all; men's nature shows itself in the worst light soon enough."

" Shall I speak to Dick ? " Mr. Highview was standing by his desk in the library, the sun shining on the top of his grey head and into his meek blue eyes, which blinked to avoid the garish light.

" *You* speak to him—what can you do ? "

" Well, not much, but I thought ——"

" Men always will think wrong."

" Sometimes a word ——."

" Fudge. It will be horribly trying and awkward. Jilted by a man in one's own county, whom by superhuman exertions one had got into Parliament, and a good *parti* too, and Luce so dreadfully plain, and she stoops worse than ever; oh dear, oh dear! how shall I ever face all the gossiping and the looks and the sneers; but men never feel for one, never, never!"

" I am sure no one can be more grieved, more disappointed than I am, but what is to be done?"

" Your niece deserves to be punished, and I hope she will be punished; the worst of it is she will punish us all too." Lady Eleanor sat down exhausted, and Mr. Highview continued to stand by the table, concerned and irresolute, wishing to help, and ignorant in what way he could render any services; foiled in his pleading and fussy in his weak anxious desire to do what was best."

" The long and the short of it is," said Lady Eleanor after a pause, " that the girl is determined to ruin her whole life, to throw away a chance and to annoy me, and I don't exactly see how it is to be helped. It is no use locking up a girl who does not care for society, and, as for starving her into submission, those things can't be done except in a novel."

" Well, certainly I should not advise starving, one might knock off a little wine or sweetmeats, girls are fond of sweetmeats; what do you think? Wine could not matter, for all the doctors are mad on the temperance question."

"That is child's play; besides, for aught we know Dick Carrol may consider himself fortunate, he was always rather wild and odd, and fond of betting and low company. That Mr. Bruce, now, was in my opinion a most dangerous adviser, a communist in an evening tie, and a very badly tied one too."

"He was a student and a quiet kind of young fellow I think, always kept his place, and seemed to listen attentively when I talked about the crops and the processes of agriculture; got that from Virgil, you know, the Georgics—almost the only Latin I ever cared for."

"Bruce must be at the bottom of all this," said Lady Eleanor firmly, "he is a social agitator, and that sort of man is always intriguing; they *must* intrigue, it is their bread and butter."

"Well, well, my dear, it is a bad business; but perhaps you are right, women have a fine instinct, a deuced fine instinct, and yet they get so taken in by their lovers, I never could understand how it is."

"You need not worry your brains about those things, I am sure; you had better help me with your refractory niece."

"I will help you, Eleanor; by this time you ought to know that I always do what I can to help you."

Lady Eleanor pouted, as much as to say "Oh, I dare say, we all know how little you can do," and swept from the room to talk the matter over with the more congenial and acuter Maud. Maud was surprised at the news of the broken engagement. She made a pretty shrewd guess at the depth of Luce's affection for Dick, and she had never for an instant supposed that a girl, however silly she might be, would, to use her own racy parlance, "cut off her nose to spite her face;" she therefore easily surmised that there was more in the affair than she could fathom.

"It is no use scolding or arguing," she said to Lady Eleanor, adding with a smile, "I know a little of womankind myself, and it is impossible to talk them into or out of love. I think with you that in a few days

Luce will bitterly regret what she has done, and probably try all in her power to get Dick back."

" And, of course, he won't come."

" There is the danger. You must try to be civil to Dick and keep on terms with him, and then there is no knowing what course events may take."

" To think that I should have to sit still and wait a girl's good pleasure," sighed Lady Eleanor, " what is the world coming to ? "

" It is deplorable," said Maud, secretly wondering whether now he was free it would be possible for her to make an impression on her cousin. She feared not. When a man has acquired indifference, no dead volcano is more difficult to rouse. And there was Arthur Sterney meanwhile engrossed with his burlesque actresses, and her youth slipping away, and her chances of marriage diminishing every day. Oh! the folly of some girls, and the wisdom of others, and the inequalities of life. It made her bitter. Presently she said, " Lady Eleanor, what do you think of change of scene ? "

" Change of scene, my dear ? "

" Yes, Luce has seen nothing of the world,

she has not yet been presented; why not give her a season in London. I am sure there is nothing to keep people in the country just now—shooting over, hunting in an expiring condition with March winds and a scarcity of foxes, and lawn tennis not yet begun—there is no hope for a girl here, and I am sure you must pine for society."

"It is certainly dull, but Luce will be of no use in London, she is so absurdly shy, and we have no town house now, you know. Since we built Highview Castle, Mr. Highview pretends he cannot afford it."

"You must coax him; he will do what you wish, I am sure."

"Well, I believe I have some influence with him," said Lady Eleanor consciously, settling her laces. She owned beautiful lace, inherited from her grandmother, and loved to display her knowledge of the differences between "point d'Alençon," "point de Venise," "appliqué," and "point d'Espagne."

"Of course no one manages better than you do. Now, Lady Eleanor, your only chance is to take a nice house in London, give dinner-parties, and cajole Dick back to your side."

"I am sure I am quite willing, but to think that I must take all this trouble for some one else's child. Doesn't it show how necessary it is for every one to have a family? Ah! Providence has not been bounteous to me, and yet I had such a fine figure when I married."

"So you have now; I never saw such beautiful shoulders as yours in an evening gown."

Lady Eleanor smiled. Certainly Maud would have suited her better than Luce.

"At any rate, Maud, you must take up your abode with us in London. Oh, I never could endure all the worry and the letter-writing unless I have you to help me; will you come?"

Maud murmured something about "my mother."

"Don't you see, your mother can let her house, and visit among her friends; that will be such an economy."

Maud saw her advantage. "But the servants, our servants are so excellent, and so obliging, we could not afford to part with them, and what would become of them?"

"You must let them with the house. Yes

indeed, it is often done; Lady Pinchwell did it last year, and so did Mrs. Friskly."

" Mrs. Friskly—but then no servants ever stay with her more than a few months."

" At any rate you must manage it; write to your mother at once, and say I desire it; she will do anything for your advantage I know, a most sensible, easy-going woman, is your mother."

Maud laughed. The impressions we convey to our friends are sometimes so strangely different from our real personalities. Maud knew her mother so thoroughly, her worldliness, her selfishness, her love of petty shifts; sensible she was certainly, with regard to seizing every scrap of material advantage, but hardly sensible in the usual acceptation of the word. However, she promised Lady Eleanor to carry out her injunctions, and volunteered to write to some house agents in London, explaining Lady Eleanor's requirements, and impressing upon them that the house in question must be large, commodious, clean, airy, warranted in a sanitary condition, and to be obtained at a low and reasonable rate.

Mr. Highview consented easily enough to

his wife's demands; he had been thoroughly
bothered and wearied by the election, and
saddened by Luce's quiet ways and pale face.
He agreed that a change would be good for
everybody. and mentally hoped that in
town the women would give him a little
peace.

CHAPTER V.

IT was some weeks after these events that Lady Fenchurch was, one day, lying on her sofa and gazing listlessly out at the tender green of the trees in the garden and park. The air was soft and balmy, filled with the gentle languor that seems to precede the more violent heats of summer, and delicately scented by the fragrant shrubs which only lately had burst into the full beauty of their blossom. It was the very day for a convalescent—bright, but not dazzling; quiet, yet not enervating. Lady Fenchurch enjoyed the weather in her languid fashion, for she was a convalescent. The nervous illness from which she had suffered since Sir Hilary's death left her weak and unstrung; a trifle startled her, a rough word set her heart beating. She was as weak as a child,

and nearly as gentle. All the impetuosity
and rebellion had been knocked out of her
by pain and sleeplessness, and Miss Fenchurch's excellent, though somewhat prosaic
and commonplace, nursing earned her a full
debt of gratitude. It was so delicious to be
well again, to feel no pain, only a pleasing
exhaustion, to be surrounded by sweet scents
and agreeable sights, and to find nothing
expected of her. Miss Fenchurch relieved
her of all cares and troubles; drilled the
servants, and visited the smallest breach of
conduct so severely that the men seemed to
walk on velvet, and the maids to handle
cups and saucers as though they were wad-
ding. No banging doors disturbed the
silence, no crashing of crockery irritated the
nerves—all was silent, peaceful, and calm.
Evelyn said little, but her grateful eyes
reassured Miss Fenchurch as to her feelings.
The good old maid wiped away a furtive
tear on the first occasion that her pale and
feeble patient smiled, for the love and attention that had once been her brother's due
she now transferred to his widow. Miss
Fenchurch was like a dog who attaches
himself to the quondam master of the house,

whoever he may be, and her days had been
passed uncomplainingly by Evelyn's bedside, in a darkened chamber, for noise and
light equally displeased the morbidly sensitive nerves of the sufferer. When the
mechanical jingling of her beloved knitting-
needles irritated Evelyn, Miss Fenchurch
uncomplainingly laid them aside for the first
time for forty years, and resigned herself to
the penance of inaction. It was, therefore,
with almost a mother's joy that the good
lady watched her charge's gradual recovery,
doubled the daily dose of wine, and increased
the luncheon from one cutlet to two, par-
taken of with proportionate appetite. The
knitting-needles were resumed, though oftener an amusing book was read aloud; and
Miss Fenchurch so far relaxed her vigilance
as to permit herself a daily walk round the
kitchen-garden, and even, after strict injunctions to the maid not to lose sight of her
mistress for one single instant, to sally down
to the farm and inquire why the butter was
not nearly as yellow as usual. During one
of these absences she had driven into West
Thorpe and ordered the prettiest and most
fashionable mourning possible, the very

mourning which had roused Lady Eleanor's sarcasm, and in thus departing from her usual contempt for dress Miss Fenchurch offered a kind of sacrificial atonement for any sins of deed and speech which might have annoyed Evelyn. And she succeeded. Lady Fenchurch was now meek and grateful, and sincerely attached to her sister-in-law. Gradually a new life returned to her, and with it a new spirit. She lay for hours motionless in her soft white tea-gown, her beautiful black eyes, liquid with gentle emotion, set wide open, thinking. Her brief married life, Sir Hilary's rage, his suspicions, his awfully sudden death, her own folly and recklessness, appeared like a dream. She was young, she was beautiful, she was free, and she stretched eagerly all the tendrils of her being towards life. It had become so precious, so valuable, life alone without conditions; the mere breathing of the air, the looking at the welcome sunshine as it slowly passed from one side of the room to the other, with ever varied effects of beauty, from pearly dawn to rosy sunset; the vivid tints of the tulips in the glasses on the table, the red melting into yellow, and yet quite

distinct; the crystalline purity and exquisite
scent of the narcissus, the drooping lily of
the valley hiding among the fresh green
leaves, delighted and enchanted her. She
felt no sorrow for Sir Hilary, no grief for
his loss; he had been a fraction, and none
too pleasant a fraction, of her former existence; but in this new life of emotion and
sentiment he had no part. She supposed
she was rich, she supposed the old house
and the good furniture and the dainty
boudoir fittings were hers; she never thought
about it; it seemed natural and right to her,
and she recked no more whence her many
comforts came, nor of the person who provided her with the luxuries her caprice
desired, than does the child inquire whether
the scullery-maid's wages be paid, or its
father's rents come in regularly. Miss Fenchurch never told her. Miss Fenchurch, to
whom all the luxury and the riches be-
longed, fed her and nursed her, and waited
upon her with the attention of a devoted
servant. The old maid could scarcely have
explained her own feelings. She required
something to pet, to manage, and provide
for. Evelyn, in her helplessness, was that

something, and afforded scope for Miss
Fenchurch's love of housekeeping, and pride
in her good housewifely skill. She did not
care for riches in themselves; her tastes were
too limited, her aspirations bounded by the
quiet home-life. But she could not abide
a speck of dust on the furniture, or a little
tarnish on the polished grates, or a silver
dish the less on the dinner-table. She would
have everything done, as she expressed it,
properly, and all these cares fully employed
her time. Miss Fenchurch was the man's
ideal woman *par excellence;* she knitted
indefatigably, and made the ordering of
dinner an elaborate study. It teazed her,
too, that Evelyn remained perfectly indifferent to the lightness of a *soufflé* or the
golden browning of a fried sole, that in the
early days of her illness she declined the most
inviting dainties, and when she grew stronger,
with the return of a healthy appetite would
eat anything indifferently from a bit of fried
bacon to a slice of roast mutton; but she
comforted herself by thinking that, though
unappreciated, the succulent dishes of her
cuisine were at least unapproachable. Miss
Fenchurch always drilled her cooks; they

began as the eldest girl in the school to learn the duties of the scullery-maid, and gradually worked their way upward to fat and comfortable mistresses of the art of cookery. To-day, profiting by the sunshine and the brilliancy of the weather, she had gone to the farm to give instructions about the slaying of a sucking-pig, for the roasting of which her cook was now famous, and thus Evelyn lay alone on her sofa, basking languidly, and enjoying the genial warmth. She had reached that state of convalescence most approaching childhood, when the animal and sensorial powers far exceed the intellectual. She enjoyed the mere fact of existence, but she wanted nothing beyond. Her thoughts were bounded by a vague wondering if Miss Fenchurch would be home to tea, and a gentle surmise as to the ending of the last new novel that lay beside her. The lovers had just been parted sharply and unaccountably, as happens in story-books, and she surmised with none too eager an interest that they would come together again in the third volume in satisfactory fashion. As though the spring sunshine had induced thoughts of love, and with them the visible presence of a lover, the door opened, and the servant inquired in a low and studiously impressive tone, whether her ladyship would receive Mr. Carrol. Lady Fenchurch had as yet received no visitors, and lying there in her loose, cream-coloured robe, could not be considered attired in orthodox widows' mourning. The servant, with the quick instinct of a lackey trained in good families, perceived this, and only the urgent insistance of the young man, and the furtive sight of a piece of gold in his hand, induced him to deliver the message. Evelyn blushed deeply. She half rose and said, " No ; I can see no one." Then, with the newly awakened appetite for change and variety and pleasing gossip, she altered her mind, and said, " Yes."

The servant, without moving a muscle of his imperturbable countenance, withdrew, and speedily admitted the visitor.

For an instant neither spoke. Evelyn was oppressed with the recollection of past events; her husband's anger and suspicion suddenly rose vividly to her mind; her hand trembled, and her lips quivered. Dick, sternly resolved on carrying out Luce's wishes, came prepared to be cold and matter-of-fact, but the vision of a beautiful woman in cool white garments, when he expected to see a tearful widow in the unbecoming black which fashion has imposed on them, lest even in hours of grief their vanity should seize the upper hand, changed the current of his thoughts, and turned indifference into admiration. After a while he recovered himself sufficiently to say:

" You have been ill ? "

" Yes, did you not know ? I have been very ill."

" Of course—the shock ——" and then he paused, while she gave a slight shudder.

" Yes, it is horrid to be a widow. I hate black."

" I see you do not wear it."

" But I shall be obliged to when I am well. You, too, are in mourning," she said, glancing at the band on his hat.

" Yes, my poor grandmother died at the time of the election."

" And now you are rich—and happy." She said this listlessly. His happiness and prosperity scarcely seemed to interest her. Dick felt piqued. We think our own affairs so all-important to others.

" Yes, I am rich and—and free."

" You are going to be married ? "

" No ; and this is why I came to see you to-day, when, perhaps, you might think it almost presumptuous in me to force my way in."

" I am glad to see you."

" You are aware of your own sad position, no doubt, and that emboldens me."

" My position ? "

" It was not my fault if circumstances were against me ; if people talked and told untruths, and if you are poor. I swear to you, Lady Fenchurch, that I never for an instant thought ——"

" You are speaking Greek to me. I cannot understand." She put up her hand to her head wearily ; it was silly of her to receive visitors; she was certainly not strong enough for the effort.

" You don't know, then ? "

" Know what ? "

" Well "—he began to stammer, evidently his action was premature—" about the will."

" Don't stammer, please—pray speak out —I hate mysteries."

" Have you not seen the will ? "

" What will ? "

" Sir Hilary's."

" No—why should I? I told you my head was not strong. I suppose it is like any other will—he left all to me, I believe."

" You are mistaken—the entailed estates go to a distant cousin, and the personalty and jewels and a large income to —— "

" Me, of course," she said complacently.

" To his sister."

" His sister! Then what is mine ? "

" Nothing, absolutely nothing ; a pittance of 400*l.* a year."

" How shameful ! " Evelyn had no practical idea of the value of 400*l.* a year; she was absolutely ignorant as to whether one could keep a carriage and horses on it, or if it would provide a good cook, but she did realise that such a sum meant comparative poverty.

" It is shameful; and then, do you see, Evelyn," he bent towards her, " people have said cruel things of you, and—do you not wish to hear ? —— "

"Go on! I can bear it all," she said, paling exceedingly. "I suppose, if this is so, I can bear it."

"And they have coupled our names together, yours and mine, and so—and so I came to say that I am at your service."

"Thank you, I dare say I can manage."

"But your character?"

"Who can say anything about it, and what do I care?"

"You are so poor, and people will not be kind to you."

"Rachel will let me live with her, I can stay here always."

"This place is only hers for a year, after that it goes away to the heir, and you will be absolutely dependent upon her: 400*l.* a year will scarcely keep you and your maid."

Evelyn stared blankly before her; why had he come in on this bright spring day, when she felt so contented and so happy, to annoy and distress her, and shatter her peace?

"Dear, I am come to say—had we not better brave these things together? I am rich, and with me by your side no one can say anything. I wanted to make you understand this soon, before you began to fret; and when your mourning is over—whenever you like—we can be married." Dick would not have spoken with the energy and generosity he now showed had Evelyn been one whit less beautiful or attractive, and had he not felt in her presence a spark of the old love revive. She was a charming and lovely widow, and at any rate he need never be ashamed of her appearance. She did not speak; he waited, but she did not speak; and lay against her cushions as white as the gown she wore.

Presently two large tears oozed from her eyes, and rolled slowly down her cheeks.

"Should you be unhappy with me, Evelyn?"

"Oh! I don't know, it is all so dreadful; why did I ever meet you? you have brought nothing but misery into my life."

When a man has just offered his hand to a woman in a fit of generosity, it is scarcely pleasant to be thus received. Dick clutched his hat and made as though he would go.

"No, no, I did not mean it," she said hurriedly, "of course I cannot mean it, only you have made me so unhappy."

"In a few months," he said, timidly touching her hand with his fingers, "when your mourning is over, we can go abroad a little, and you will forget."

"I suppose I shall," she answered with an accent of indolent despair. "I dare say you are right."

The wooing was certainly not very satisfactory; Dick's success could scarcely be said to lie in love, but Evelyn was beautiful, and Luce had said it was his duty. Spite of all, the thought of her, and of what she desired, formed the motive power of his conduct.

"Then it is settled, we are engaged." She bowed her head, and he printed a passionless kiss on her white forehead. "I shall not call again, it is better not; I must guard your reputation now, it is my care."

"Ah ! what does a woman not endure for the sake of her reputation ?" said Evelyn wearily, turning a little away from him.

"I am not disagreeable to you surely ?" he said in a tone of pained surprise, "remember you are quite free, you must please yourself."

"Oh no, you are very kind, and I am not

well, and besides you know I cannot be gay, I am in mourning."

" I quite understand ; you might write to me occasionally and look upon me as your friend, and if you wish to see me I will come, but not otherwise ; we must be careful, only now you know you are neither defenceless nor dependent." He rose and lingered a little as if he expected some warmer response, but she only said, " Thank you. I will not forget, and I will write to you—of course I may tell Rachel ? "

" Of course, but we had better keep it a secret from everyone else, people would say it was too soon."

" Yes. Are you at Long Leam ? "

" For a few days only. My uncle and aunt are still there. What is a bachelor to do in a big house by himself ? "

" I can't imagine," she said indifferently. Then, as the pause became embarrassing, he bowed, and left the room. The strange wooing was scarcely over when Miss Fen-church returned brimful of news about the sucking-pig.

" Such a beauty, my dear, and Mrs. Hodges says it was the finest litter we have had this year. I do hope you will have appetite enough to eat it; the cook's stuffing is always good, and apples are still plentiful, though it is late for them. You look pale; now I dare say you've never taken your quinine, I will ring for it at once, and there's a dreadful draught from that window, you should have put on a shawl."

CHAPTER VI.

Bruce, when for an instant he allowed his thoughts to stray away from the great work which was now nearing something like completion (the first volume being finished, and the last proof-sheets just passing through the press), sometimes thought of the strangely pleasant time he had spent at Highview, and of the pale girl with the large brown eyes, in whose company he had passed many hours. She was so different to her surroundings, so still, and so introspective, qualities which he had not hitherto found characteristic of the fashionable world, that he often wondered what her life was, and her feelings. It sometimes occurred to him as singular that she should have engaged herself to Dick, but he rapidly dismissed this thought with the reflection that no doubt girls in her position were brought up to look upon marriage as a purely business relation, and the choice of a husband as a commercial affair. Still it grated upon his feelings. Luce had appeared to him so thoroughly womanly, so feminine in her words and movements, so formed for a deep attachment, even for passion, that he could not help fancying she would suffer in a *mariage de convenance*. The glimpse of idle life he had caught at Highview scarcely impressed him with a sense of pleasure; fine dinners and a show of gold plate wearied him, while the beauty of their dress, and the sprightliness of their manners, rather heightened the effect of the vapidity of great people. In the library however, neglected and un-disturbed, he had been very happy, very happy also in his fireside talks with Luce. For the first time in his life, he associated on terms of familiar equality, aided by an already acquired friendliness due to Dick's praises, with a charming woman of a refined and cultivated mind. The only two other women he habitually saw, his landlady and his own mother, could not be said to stand in this kind of relation to him; a mother, whatever her peculiarities, is always one's

mother, and therefore sacred, and a landlady
of the gushing order is preferably kept at a
distance, therefore the free and gentle inter-
change of sentiments and opinions he had
enjoyed with Luce, bore a doubly precious
meaning. Bruce scarcely realised it at the
time; he fancied the sole privilege he
enjoyed at Highview was the run of the
library, and the unique opportunity of study-
ing some old fifteenth-century manuscripts,
black-letter type, and "l'Estoile's Journals
of Henry III. and Henry IV."; but when
he returned to his lonely lodging, his work,
and his brightly-burning, if somewhat un-
pleasantly smelling, student's lamp, he
missed something—and only after days of
discomfort and uneasiness did he realise that
that something was a woman's face. Once
even he leant back in his chair, interrupting
a vivid description of Anglo-Saxon manners
he was writing, to weave a day-dream.
The dream of a gentle voice by his side, a
sweet face at his elbow, ready to assist and
encourage; overcoming difficulties with a
smile, and clearing away despondencies by a
laugh; then when the work was finished,
and put away for the nonce, of a pair of

loving arms wrapped about his weary
shoulders, and of words of love murmured in
his ear. It was for this no doubt that he
had lived a life of solitude, endured long
hours of silent monotony, toiled and suffered
alone. He crossed his arms, and a smile
played about his mouth. Woman's love, the
crown and glory of life, the ideal beauty of
all things, the passage of an angel's wings
on earth! People said that passion weakened
a man; that to be strong it was necessary
to stand alone. He felt this as a fallacy:
union was strength, and love was nothing if
not a fusion of human lives. He pleased
himself occasionally with these musings.
The woman's face was always Luce, the
woman's voice always her soft contralto.
He had kept aloof so long from the ephemeral
and sensual passions that beset men, that he
was the veriest tyro in matters of love,
but for that very reason, perhaps, better
qualified to taste and appreciate. But,
though the woman of whom he dreamt bore
the presentment of the only girl he had
known well, yet he never for one single
instant thought of her as owning a personal
relation to him, even before he heard of her

engagement, and naturally afterwards such a thing became impossible. He only dwelt upon her image as the poet and the artist revels in picture-galleries or among splendid works of sculpture, which do not belong to him, in which he has no actual part, but yet which he makes his own by right of sympathy and æsthetic comprehension. Immersed in his studies, he had heard nothing of the Highview establishment since the election—indeed, had seen but little of Luce at that time, and his surprise was only equalled by his sympathy, when Dick informed him of the abrupt termination to his engagement.

"She wished you to be free, she gave you no reason," he said, meditatively, scratching with his pen on the blotting-paper.

"Yes, she gave a reason—a woman's reason." Dick stretched himself on the narrow sofa, his heels in the air. "Said I had compromised somebody else; and so must marry that somebody. A stupid solution, if ever there was one."

"Miss Windermere is usually reasonable."

"So I always thought; she was firm

G 2

enough, obstinate enough, in all conscience, but she was certainly not reasonable."

"It is strange."

"She never thought of my feelings, though she pretended to love me; it is no more pleasant for a man than for a woman to be jilted, one feels such a fool. Besides, what am I to do in a big house by myself? and I could not stand those Vincents."

"But in giving you your freedom I suppose she thought she was acting rightly."

"I suppose she did. Women are so extraordinary."

"You will carry out her wishes?"

"Deuce take me if I want to carry out anybody's wishes but my own, and look round a little. I've been so worried."

"And what will become of Miss Windermere?"

"How can I tell? She'll marry some other fellow, I suppose; or become an old maid. It's her own doing entirely."

Bruce thought for a moment, leaning his head on his hand. Presently he said:

"Yes, women *are* extraordinary. It passes my comprehension how, in life, one seems to come quite close to people, to breathe the same air, to think the same thoughts, to partake of their very nature, and then to drift away apart as if one had never met, or seen, or loved, the one person who, for a short time, has been everything in the world to one, dearer and closer than heart had ever conceived. Once you loved Lady Fenchurch in this fashion."

"But she deceived me—she led me on and treated me like a boy—no man can stand that."

"And then came Miss Windermere."

"I never pretended to love her."

"And you meant to marry, not loving? What a fatal, what a terrible mistake."

"I don't know; she suited me very well, she understood me fairly, she did not rub me up or reproach me—no man of spirit can stand reproaches—she gave me my *congé* very nicely too."

"Would you be surprised to learn that in doing her duty, as she believed it, she did violence to her own feelings; no woman parts quietly with a man unless she loves him still; one does not parley with a ferocious beast, but one lets a dove flutter and fly and return to the hand that fed it."

" Thank you for the simile, a ferocious wild beast. I've certainly no luck with women."

" Possibly the women believe they have no luck with you."

" Luce was a fool. I should have made a remarkably kind husband."

"And run after every other pretty woman that came in your way."

" Don't imagine that the privilege of friendship gives you the right to lecture. I object to personal observations."

" Seriously, Dick, I'm sorry for this *contre-temps*, but Miss Windermere is an intelligent girl. If she advised you to give her up and to return to your old love it was no doubt because she saw the wisdom of the proceeding."

Dick bit his moustache.

" I declare I think I shall marry no one; and yet to live in a big house by oneself is horrid; I hate solitude and coming home to find one's fire out and not a soul to speak to."

" Oh, you had much better marry," said Bruce, from among his folios. "And a widow may possibly be equal to restraining your impetuosity."

"I wish you wouldn't talk like that—impetuosity indeed—but it's early days to talk of a widow. She is scarcely out of her first mourning."

"A widow's mourning is like a girl's coyness—put on to allure."

"I declare you are growing cynical."

"The effect of these barbaric old Anglo-Saxons upon a weary brain, I suppose. And so you don't regret Miss Windermere?"

"Regret! I'm thoroughly disgusted."

"But you're not breaking your heart?"

"Breaking my heart, no. I very nearly did that once."

"And you've bought your experience—come, you see you're getting on—in your next love affair you won't move a muscle. Practice makes perfect."

"You are intolerable. I shall go out."

"Do. Smoke a cigarette, chew a toothpick, and go to lunch with some pretty little girl; by tea-time you will have forgotten Miss Windermere's very existence, and be quite ready for another affair."

Dick disdained to answer, clapped his hat on his head, and left the room, slamming

the door. Bruce buried his face in his hands
and heaved something like a sigh.

"He does not regret her; a girl who is far
too good for him, who is breaking her own
heart while she tries to heal another's; a girl
who has feeling and sense, and modesty and
a *heart*—and all this thrown away on a
fatuous idiot who talks of marrying because
he is lonely in a big house—lonely indeed!—
he can drink, and smoke, and play billiards,
and what will she do? I can see her with
her soft brown eyes full of tears, and her
voice like a summer wind, telling him not
to think of her—Ah! I have no patience, the
idiots, the idiots there are, and I myself am
the greatest idiot of all. What is it to me?
He will marry the widow, and they will have
plenty of money, and give dinners, and
bring up a large family of sportsmen and
dancing, flirting women, and *she* will find
someone else to her taste, a coronet perhaps,
or some great squire, and one day I shall see
her face at the opera, with a sweet little
child by her side, or meet her driving calm
and unruffled in the Park, and neither he
nor she will ever remember." He clenched
his hands angrily, and his pale cheek grew

paler.   His friends, the few he cared to see,
said he worked too much ; his long fingers
grew transparent, one could see the veins
through them, and he stooped more, and his
cheeks grew haggard.   A pretty fellow he
to think of women and to dream of love. He
said to himself angrily that he didn't dream
of love, but that as a philosopher he had a
perfect right to note and classify the various
phases of human folly.   There was a girl
now, cultivated, modest, gentle, high-minded,
giving up the man she loved (Bruce made a
shrewd guess at the state of her feelings) for
an idea of honour which few men would
have heeded.   There was honour then in
women, they were not all " at heart a rake,"
not all mercenary and worldly in her rank
of life.   The study of a woman's heart was
as much a study as any other —it represented
a type and had a decided ethical purpose.
How much of the individual could be traced
to the inherited prejudices of progenitors,
how much to habit, how much to education,
and what was left of the individual when all
these various influences were removed and
discarded ?   Would the consciousness of
right-doing support her in her sacrifice, or

would her woman's feebleness and yearning for affection cause her to suffer? Which would suffer most, she in her trampling down of natural feeling for an impossible ideal, he in his future disillusion? Bruce tried to argue out these thoughts like a metaphysical problem, he endeavoured to frame them in abstract form, and all the while he felt that the girl was right, far more right than he had ever conceived possible. He turned with assiduous ardour to his notes, his authorities, his manuscripts, and tried to drown his newly awakened interest in the present by an increased absorption in the past; but the black-letter swam before his eyes, the Anglo-Saxon flowed into modern English; the old dry bones clothed themselves in flesh and blood, the ancient forms and expressions changed into modern commonplace, and always a girl's voice disturbed his labours and a girl's eyes looked through the crabbed writing of the musty papers. "I am ill," he said to himself, rising abruptly; "too much learning hath made thee mad. I must buy a bicycle and join the ranks of happy shop-boys careering on a Saturday half-holiday into the country. It is the spring coming on, my room is stifling, and there is a thrush singing in the tree outside my window."

Dick did not call again for some time and Bruce was glad of it. He did not wish to hear more of his friend's love affairs, they were annoying and interrupting to a man engaged in a great work. Dick's sphere and his were not the same. He had always held it as a mistake for people to try and lift themselves out of the class in which they were born; he was one of the people, he was proud of it, the dominion of the intelligence was well understood to be greater than the power of wealth and rank. He could not imagine any one priding himself on birth, for birth is an accident, while merit is a claim. He should claim his due some day, but it would not be in idle and fashionable society.

CHAPTER VII.

A few days later, Bruce was walking down
one of the tolerably quiet streets leading
out of Oxford Street. He had been to fetch
a book from the London Library, and was
returning to his lodgings to digest it at his
leisure. Absorbed in thought of the intellectual treat in store for him, he strode along,
as was his wont, with head bent down, and
meditative eyes fixed on the ground. Suddenly a smart victoria with a pair of splashing horses, and a couple of supercilious, well-
dressed servants on the box, pulled up beside
the pavement. Startled, he lifted his eyes,
and saw Lady Eleanor, smiling and well-
dressed, beckoning to him, and Luce by her
side. At first he thought it a mistake. So
fashionable a lady could have nothing to say

to a poor student, shabbily dressed, and carrying a book under his arm. He knew his position, he did not mean to trangress it; a business visit in company of the man he was coaching in political matters constituted no title to social intimacy, when all the conditions were reversed. He paused, and glanced round to observe if there were no one else in sight, for whom the greeting was designed. No, only a young dressmaker hurrying along with a parcel, and two working-men carrying tools, were in sight. Lady Eleanor waved her hand again, and presently the powdered footman approached, and said her ladyship wished to speak with him. Bruce advanced to the carriage.

"Really Mr. Bruce," said her ladyship in her most affable manner, "we have had so much trouble to attract your attention I positively thought you did not wish to acknowledge us."

Bruce bowed. "Your ladyship could scarcely believe that, but I was in doubt whether your greeting was intended for me."

"Of course; we nodded, and waved our hands violently, didn't we Luce? not that you ever do anything violently, you're too indifferent; " this in an undertone, which however Bruce, whose faculties were quickened, heard distinctly. He thought Luce paler than ever, and there were certainly dark rings under her eyes, which told of pain or sleeplessness, but she gave him one of her sweetest and most encouraging smiles. After that, he prepared to listen attentively to Lady Eleanor's garrulousness.

"We have been in town some time; you must come and see us; Eaton Square you know. I always like a square because it is quiet and one can breathe. I suppose you are in town?"

" I am always in town."

" Then we shall expect you. Sunday is the best time to find us in; every other day there is something going on, and now there's Hurlingham on Saturday. I am really tired to death of all the whirl and the tea-parties. These afternoons with music are most tedious; but what can one do? One must behave like every one else, or one is soon left behind."

" It must be fatiguing." Bruce spoke to Lady Eleanor, but he looked steadfastly at

Luce, who sat there so quiet and silent, a kind of impassive veiled prophetess in the volatile rattle and business of her fashionable aunt.

"Fatiguing? I should think so—it's simply killing. Do you ever go to parties?"

"Never."

"Never? Fancy living in London without going to parties; one might as well be buried in the ruins of Pompeii, and see skeletons and petrified bread all round one. Then there's art, too, one owes so much to that—the Grosvenor, and the Academy, and the Watercolour Institute. I go to all the private views, and all the first nights at the theatre, and I attend sales of china and old prints and pictures. I'm a great collector, you know ——" Here Lady Eleanor paused for breath.

"I remember your ladyship had a number of beautiful things at Highview Castle."

"I should think so. I have quite as good china as the Rothschilds, and I'm always picking up bargains. Now, only the other day ——"

"And does Miss Windermere enjoy all this gaiety very much?" said Bruce, uncourteously interrupting Lady Eleanor's effusion. His question immediately set her off on another subject, and she answered for her niece.

"It's her first season, you know. Oh, yes, all girls like going out, though Luce is very quiet about everything; but she enjoys it, don't you, Luce?"

"Very much, aunt," answered Luce gently, with a droop of her eyelids.

"I imagine a season in London is something like a man's first campaign; it brings out all the qualities and capacities of his nature."

"It brings out every one's temper. You wouldn't believe what a trial servants are now, especially in the season, when one requires such attention."

"Of course," said Bruce, absently watching Luce's little gloved hands which moved nervously.

"By-the-bye," said Lady Eleanor, with that easy adaptability to change which is the characteristic of fashionable society, "have you seen anything of your friend Mr. Carrol? We have not set eyes on him lately; how is he, do you know? Immersed in politics, I suppose? I wonder if he is going to vote for woman suffrage."

Luce blushed, a rosy red, she could not help it. Bruce's eyes seemed to look her through and through, and to note each varying emotion of her poor little heart. He discreetly removed his gaze from her now, however; he hated to see the child blush and involuntarily reveal her sorrow and her suffering. Lady Eleanor saw that he was not attending to her discourse, and became impatient. She always liked to be first in every man's consideration.

" *Have* you seen Mr. Carrol?" she asked, tartly.

Bruce, suddenly recalled to reason, blurted out an incoherent answer, that Dick was in town, he believed, and very busy with the House, but that he didn't exactly know what he was doing.

" Very well, then, don't forget your promise; come and see us soon, and tell us about him—on Sunday, you know." She signed to the servant to drive on, and Luce moved her lips as if to say farewell, but no sound escaped them.

" And that girl loved him," Bruce muttered to himself, as he stood on the pavement watching the carriage drive off; then he shifted his book to the other arm and walked away. The lodgings seemed stuffier and dingier than ever when he returned. Mrs. Flinks and her smiles and ogles, and even her boxes of stocks and mignonette in the window, emitting a fragrant odour, in which the widow's soul delighted, vexed and irritated him.

He climbed to his lonely room and threw himself on the sofa. "Shall I visit them?" he thought, and then the sense of equality, which lies dormant in the breast of every Englishman, rose up within him, and he said, "Yes—why not—I am their equal in brains, in knowledge, in capacity." But he was not their equal in riches and position, and he was too wise not to know this, and to feel how heavily the want of these things handicapped him. Notwithstanding, after a few days he decided to avail himself of Lady Eleanor's invitation and to call in Eaton Square on the following Sunday. Lady Eleanor herself, very properly, cared nothing about the penniless student (if people were born poor it was their misfortune, she could

not be expected to redress the inequalities of
fortune), but she still fondly hoped for
Dick's return, and she believed that in
attracting Bruce to her house she was cul-
tivating a bond of union between her and
the recreant lover. Bruce was certain to
talk to Dick of his visit (probably he seldom
had a chance of calling on titled ladies living
in Eaton Square), might kindle by his enthusiastic descriptions the dwindling flame
of love; might create a desire in Dick to see
again the girl he had so nearly married. All
this in the flash of inspiration passed through
Lady Eleanor's brain, when she stopped the
carriage to speak to Bruce, a condescension
she would not otherwise have been guilty
of, and she determined to be extremely
gracious to the student and to encourage his
visits; arguing, that with so unworldly and
inexperienced a person it would not be difficult to obtain some influence, and to mould
him to her wishes.

Bruce had taken extra pains with his
toilet on the occasion of this visit; lank and
ungraceful he could not help appearing, but
his long white hands with the filbert-shaped
nails, his quiet, refined manner, and high in-

telligent forehead, procured for him, at least,
a certain amount of distinction.   He was a
man you could not help noticing, and, except
perhaps to some very young and silly girl,
he would prove more interesting than the
cloud of ordinary mashers, with their chok-
ingly tight collars and groom-like habili-
ments.   Lady Eleanor smiled graciously
upon him when he entered her stately drawing-room, set out with all the bric-a-brac she
was insatiable in buying, but after a word
or two waved him off with vague amiability,
while she addressed some other more ele-
gantly attired guest.   Bruce drifted away a
little into a corner, rather helplessly wondering what he should do next, when Luce's
soft voice desired him to come and sit beside
her.   She made one of a knot of girls and
men talking and laughing, amongst whom
Bruce recognised Maud Hardfast and Arthur
Sterney.   Maud greeted him in her bold,
hearty fashion.

"Fancy you here, Mr. Bruce.   I thought
you never stirred from your books."

"Not often, I confess, but on Sunday
even I, require a little relaxation."

"It is too hot to exert oneself," sighed

Maud, leaning gracefully back in her chair (illnatured people declared she studied every one of these idle, careless poses before the looking-glass). " I declare it's the hottest June I ever remember."

" I delight in warm weather," said Luce.

" I shouldn't think those wretched men who have to sit up all night in the House appreciate it much," put in Maud, viciously. " I declare, when one comes home from a ball, tired out, and sees that light burning, and remembers that those poor creatures are still at it, squabbling over a cattle disease bill, or sparring with a tiresome government official, and obliged to sit there all the time whether they like it or not, it gives one the shudders. I am so glad I am not a man, and especially not an M.P., aren't you Mr. Bruce ? "

" Well, you see, I am not a fair judge. I *am* a man, though not an M.P."

" Of course, that is what I meant. And how is your friend Dick Carrol ? I always promised him I would go and hear his first speech in the House, and, of course, I never did," she said, turning round with a laugh to attract Arthur Sterney's approbation.

"I believe Carrol is doing very well, and takes a great interest in politics, but I have not seen him lately."

"Not seen him lately?" asked Maud, curiously; "have you two quarrelled, then? You used to be like a pair of twins, or Orestes and Pylades, those two absurd friends one reads about in the schoolroom."

Luce leant a little forward listening.

Bruce said in a grave voice, "I do not generally quarrel, but when one is very busy —one has less time to spare for the claims of friendship. Cannot you imagine two people meeting only rarely, and yet taking up their intimacy exactly at the point they left off whenever they do meet?"

"No, I can't. I forget people if I don't see them constantly. Most women do—I think."

"Is that your opinion, Miss Windermere?" said Bruce, turning to her with a suppressed light in his eye.

"I don't know, I am sure. I think it is difficult to forget."

"There's one thing, duns never forget," laughed Arthur Sterney; "my bootmaker sends me in his bill every month, and I regularly file it. I assure you I am most business-like."

"But you are very extravagant," said Maud, looking at him tenderly through her half-closed lids.

"I hate a screw," said the young guardsman. "I know fellows who would rather buy a sixpenny button-hole than go without. I'm quite different; the best of everything is good enough for me, and I never wear anything but a gardenia or a clove carnation; everything else is only fit for cads."

"I wonder what a man's flower-bill comes to, and his cigars, at the end of the year!" mused Maud; "I expect it would pay for a good many of our dresses."

"Do you ever wear sixpenny flowers?" asked Sterney of Bruce, who was listening with a smile of amusement.

"Never!" responded the latter. "I can't bear anything of inferior quality; if I haven't a gardenia I go without."

"Quite right," said the guardsman, on whom the implied sarcasm was totally wasted.

Lady Eleanor now approached. "Mrs. Straightly wants us to go down to Eton on the 4th of June," she said to Maud; "what do you think—can we manage it?"

"Oh, pray do," urged Mrs. Straightly, a smartly dressed matron with unwarrantably golden hair. "I promised poor little Willie, and I can't go alone. This is his first year at Eton, you know."

"Eton is going to the dogs," murmured Arthur Sterney, sententiously; "it isn't the same place at all, ever since all the rich snobs and their sons have gone there, and they've done away with fighting and caning; they want some of the good stand-up fights they used to have; the boys ain't half plucky, and the masters are always putting it down— make 'em into a lot of milk-sops if they go on; as if it wasn't natural to boys to fight and get black eyes; they enjoy it, and a good licking does 'em a world of good occasionally."

"I'm glad I'm not a boy," shuddered Maud.

"Oh, you'd like it if you were at school."

"What a lovely style of workbasket that is of yours, Lady Eleanor!" pursued Mrs. Straightly, dropping the subject of Eton boys; "something quite new, I am sure, and *so French*."

" Yes, I flatter myself it is pretty," said her hostess, turning the basket round that it might be admired on all sides; " Madame Mousseline got it for me."

" Ah, then, I was right; I thought it was French."

The combination of barbaric splendour with a homely article intended for homely purposes might have been French, but was certainly incongruous; but to some minds a thing, however ugly, if unusual, is pleasing, and the highest form of praise that can be given seems to be " so French." A book, or a dress, or a play, or a person, or a senti-ment, all are equally applicable; to modern ears it has the sound of a word which highly delighted our grandmothers, " vastly pretty." In mincing style and tightly drawn back skirt a lady now says "so French!" where in pelisse and tippet she would have formerly murmured with a curtsey, " Ah, how vastly pretty," " Sir, I am vastly obliged."

Mrs. Straightly presently moved away, accompanied by Lady Eleanor, whose digni-fied manner of receiving, highly gratified those who were not so sure of their own dignity. Maud commenced whispering behind her fan with Arthur Sterney, and Bruce was left almost alone beside Luce.

"Did I hear you say you had seen nothing of Mr. Carrol?" she asked, tremulously.

"Nothing."

"I should like to know ——" she began, and then stopped abruptly.

"Can I find out anything for you? I am at your service," he said, in a grave, resonant voice. Luce liked his voice. In nothing, perhaps, is character and education more noticeable than in that. No educated person leaves out his h's, or speaks with a broad and vulgar accent, and yet individuality is revealed in a marvellous degree by the tones of the voice. Bruce spoke like a thinker, in somewhat slow and measured accents, and yet with a lilt and a nice sense of gradation that proved he had been accustomed to say things worth listening to, and not merely to fritter away an idle hour in small-talk.

"Don't you think you ought to see Mr. Carrol?" said Luce presently.

"Why? For my sake or for his?"

" For his ; you are such a friend."

" As long as I was of service to him he could count upon me, but now he is happy ; he is fortunate and rich, and has a career— perhaps he would only deem me imper- tinent."

" And do you think the fortunate do not want friends quite as much as the unfor- tunate ?   Ah, you are mistaken there."

" The fortunate can always *find* friends ; they do not need to seek them like the unhappy."

" It is sometimes difficult to define happi- ness, and I am sure no one is so perfectly happy as never to need a friend.   I don't think you appreciate Mr. Carrol as much as you did."

" Indeed, you are mistaken, but ——"

" But what ?   You look mysterious."

" It is not always advisable to say all that one thinks."

ᐧLuce remained silent ; she felt that it would savour of forwardness if she discussed Mr. Carrol's friendships any longer.   After all, what was he to her ?   She had no more right to offer even an opinion.   She sighed.

" And do you like this life ? "   Bruce

asked, emboldened by the sigh; "does it satisfy and please you?"

"It is a good thing to see varieties of life," she said; "girls know so little of *real* life; they never see it except through the medium of expediency and social prejudice."

" And a roseate hue is perhaps as good a one as any other to view objects through."

" You used not to talk like that formerly; you used to say that one ought to try and find out the truth of things, and only see them exactly as they were without reticence or idealisation."

"Did I? And suppose I found I was wrong."

" Oh no; it can never be wrong to seek for the right; just think, if there were no real right, and one had sacrificed everything for a shadow."

" That would indeed be unfortunate, but it is not likely; the scales would probably not fall from one's eyes in that case."

" And how is the book progressing?" said Luce, changing the subject, which she felt was likely to become personal.

" Very well, thank you; but, strange to say, I am getting a little tired of work."

" You ? "

" Yes, I.   Did you think I was a nature-bred slave and loved my chains ? "

" I thought you a man likely to do great things."

"Thank you.   Well, I suppose it is wrong and weak, but sometimes I feel inclined to throw away my manuscripts, my ink, and my pen, and to go right away somewhere, and lead a ruminating life under blue skies, lie in a cowslip meadow, or some sweet, quiet, lazy place."

" You are overworked."

" Do you think so ; do you really think a man ought never to sigh for relaxation, for pleasure, for innocent pleasure, or do you think I am constituted differently from other men and am only a machine ? "

" I never thought that," she said, looking distressed.   Just then Maud rose and began a prolonged leave-taking of Arthur Sterney, interspersed with joking recommendations and laughing rejoinders, and allusions which were incomprehensible to any but the initiated.   He rose also, and stood silently in a stiff attitude, wondering whether he ought to bring his visit to a close.   This problem was solved for him by Lady Eleanor, who, released from her attendance on other guests, beckoned him to her side and insisted on his drinking a cup of scalding tea. This occupation and Lady Eleanor's stream of talk diverted his attention from Luce; and he left the house dissatisfied with himself and the interrupted conversation.

CHAPTER VIII.

SOME days elapsed: Bruce did not return, and nothing was heard of Dick. Maud, happily engaged in a chaffy kind of flirtation with Arthur Sterney, for whom the burlesque actresses had temporarily lost their charm, scarcely noticed Luce's preoccupation; and yet Luce was extremely preoccupied. Since that day of the parting in the shrubbery Dick had never written to her, she was entirely ignorant of his doings, and uneasy lest in cutting him loose from herself she had sent him adrift into the world. If he should not feel sufficiently bound in honour to offer his hand to Lady Fenchurch, if Lady Fenchurch herself were to refuse him, if disgusted and fancy-free he were to plunge into excesses and dissipation, would not the consequences fall upon Luce? He had assured her of his intention to lead a quiet, country gentleman's life, to retrench, and to be charitable to his neighbours; he had evinced sufficient inclination for her to be easy on the score of his kindly treatment of her, but she had ungratefully destroyed all these good intentions, and thrown over his budding virtues the cold frost of her own withdrawal. She had meant well, truly, she had believed herself to be acting rightly, but that was not enough if it could be proved that she had *not* acted rightly. The very sensitiveness of Luce's conscience tormented and robbed her of tranquillity and happiness. It might be possible to imagine a condition of contented serenity, on which the consciousness of self-sacrifice should confer a double lustre, a state of rapt spirituality, where the spirit of the martyr left no space for the pains of the body; but to crawl wearily through life, feeling one had sacrificed one's own bliss quite unnecessarily for purely abstract idea of duty, resulting only in remote and unimportant consequences, was neither comforting nor flattering to the mind of a young girl, as anxious as her neighbours to extract all that was plea-

sant out of this weary journey on earth.
Luce was no saint, and she had none
of that impassioned fervour which keeps
some people from ever suspecting that their
own decisions can be wrong. She had hoped
to hear something reassuring from Bruce,
and to her additional annoyance it seemed
as though a breach had come between the
two friends. It was about this time, the
season being now well advanced, and the
lime-trees shedding a sweet fragrance over
the languid riders in Rotten Row, that Luce,
riding beside her uncle one day, caught sight
of Dick. He was looking remarkably well,
and was mounted on a handsome horse.
Beside him was a lady, a young lady, and
on the other side an older man, evidently
her father. He immediately recognised
Luce and her uncle, smiled, and bowed pleasantly. But he continued his placid ride
beside the young lady, and showed no inclination to approach his ex-betrothed. Luce
coloured violently, but strove to conceal it,
hoping that a scarlet face might be placed
to the account of the broiling sun.

"Ah! there's Carrol," remarked Mr.
Highview, shaking his fist familiarly at him,

as is the wont of men when they recognise an acquaintance. "It's the first time I've seen him riding—a very good-looking chesnut, too, shows some breeding; he's fond of horses; I shouldn't wonder if he took the hounds next year. He'd make a first-rate master."

"Yes," murmured Luce, anxious to say something and appear unconcerned, but unable to find a fitting remark.

"He spoke in the House the other night, and very properly, too, I am told."

"What was the subject?" ventured Luce, tapping her horse nervously with her riding-whip.

"It was a small affair, that pigeon shooting business, got up by a lot of sentimentalists; but I believe Dick spoke in a very moderate and gentlemanly way."

"Do you know who was the young lady riding with him?" asked Luce presently.

"No, I don't. But I recognised the man as a rich ironmaster, who is in the House, Member for —— Oh, I forget the name, somewhere in the Midlands."

"And that was his daughter, I suppose?"

"Probably. Shall we canter on? If we

meet Dick again I'll ask him to luncheon,
that is to say, if you don't mind, my dear?"

"I don't mind," she said, feebly, and they
started off. But Dick never appeared again,
and Luce returned home with a bitter pain
at her heart. An ironmaster's daughter, a
rich girl, a pretty girl too, as far as she
could judge by the slight figure, and the
golden locks neatly coiled under the black
riding-hat. A spasm of jealousy shook her.
It was not for this she had surrendered him.
Not that he should play the butterfly, and
perhaps marry the first silly girl he happened
to meet.

Why had he not turned his horse's head
and spoken to her—just one word? He knew
her well enough to surmise how kindly she
would receive him. She had not reckoned on
the strength of a man's vanity, which causes
him to forgive an injury sooner than a slight.
She forgot that though her feelings towards
Dick were not changed, yet that his feelings
towards her could no longer be the same.
Even though he did not love her, he could
resent her withdrawing her promise, and
offering him advice.

And so she fretted herself nearly ill over

Dick's neglect, fancying, like the foolish girl she was, that a man would remain her friend whom she had refused as a lover. A man's self-esteem is the last of all his passions to die out. And while Dick rode with Miss Denvil, as a pure pastime, thinking her a jolly unaffected girl, and impressed with the conviction that her father's champagne was excellent, once she was out of his sight he never bestowed an instant's further consideration upon her, Luce, racked by unreasoning acute jealousy, shed copious tears over his fickleness, as she called it, and passed a sleepless night. Oh, happy time of youth, when a look or a word from one we love has power to change the current of our thoughts, to transport us from Hell into Paradise, to cloud a brilliant sky, or make the roses of happiness grow in the dull wintry weather! Happy torments, happy aches and anguish, which the oldest of us would not exchange for the dull disillusion and stony unfeelingness of mature life! These transports, these anticipations, these disappointments, these doubtings and despairs, are of the essence of love and youth, no placid certitude can ever take their place.

Lady Eleanor, who had been informed of the meeting in the park by Mr. Highview, rallied Luce on her depression, and endeavoured by taunts and ridicule to rouse her pride and create regret.

"It is your conduct, my dear," she said, as they swayed to and fro, in uncomfortable position, in the string of carriages that formed the approach to a popular ball, "that has driven away young Carrol, and now I hear he is always riding about with Miss Denvil, a sensible girl; she will not refuse him, her father made his money in trade, and she intends to marry well. Good gracious! what a jerk," as her jewelled head was nearly propelled against Luce's shoulder; "this kind of thing is dreadful, it makes me feel sick."

"You should not come for my sake, aunt," replied Luce, earnestly; "you know I don't care for balls."

"Nonsense, child; it is my duty." Duty or not, Lady Eleanor would sooner have nodded and swayed in her carriage for a full hour, as the trying prelude to a night's dissipation, than have spent one single, quiet evening at home.

" But, as I said," proceeded Lady Eleanor as soon as she had settled her *coiffure*, " you have entirely spoilt your own chances. I suppose you are pleased, as it is your own handiwork, and you think yourself remarkably clever. For my part I can't conceive anything more ridiculous than a girl handing over her lover to another girl, who has more money than herself, and thus forcing him to do a mercenary action, which she chooses to qualify by the name of sacrifice."

Luce bit her lips. This transcription of her own wretched thoughts was bitter enough in all conscience.

" Real love to my mind implies mutual sacrifice. I never knew anybody who was in love who did not desire some return for her feelings. But you are a cold, hard girl, I have always known it; you never cared for me, and yet I have done everything to gain your affections."

" Oh, aunt ! how can you say such cruel things ?" answered Luce, in much distress.

" I wish I could say more cruel things, and make you see your absurd conduct in a true light. You think yourself a heroine, your friends look upon you as a fool."

Luce winced. Had she not believed the same thing herself in the solitude of her own room and the perfect confidence of her pillow?

" What good will it do you to be laughed at as an old maid, to grow sallower and sallower—old maids always enjoy headaches, and bad health—to live in cheap lodgings, and go out to high tea in a cab, to keep a frowsy maid of all work who steals the sugar, and takes your writing-paper to indite notes to her young man? If that is the fate you prefer, to being the wife of one of the richest and handsomest young men in the county, I think I can assure you, you have every chance of attaining it."

A silent tear rolled down Luce's cheek. She must plunge into society, she must endeavour to forget. Much as she had shrunk from crowds, and avoided assemblies, so much the more now would she pursue pleasure in hot haste. The best nun is she who has a fault to expiate, they say; the best trifler, the most ardent devotee of fashion, is the woman who tries to forget, to drown sorrow in amusement. Luce dried her tears, and contrived to make herself so

agreeable to her partners at the ball, that
Lady Eleanor regarded her with a smile of
approbation. Her animated manner, the
unusual colour in her cheek, her somewhat
reckless talk, transformed the quiet, almost
ordinary young person, whose smiles were
sparse, and whose interest was only given to
those worthy of attention, into a lively,
frivolous girl. This was a change that
delighted Lady Eleanor, and she promised
herself to renew her sarcastic remarks, since
the result had already proved so satisfactory.

CHAPTER IX.

DICK meanwhile plunged into politics, as
Luce had done into pleasure. Lord Lytton
truly says, " Who does not know what
active citizens our private misfortunes make
us." The mind must find something on
which to exercise its energies; foiled in
love, a man naturally turns to ambition, and
Dick was slowly and painfully acquiring a
taste for the government of his country. It is
a matter for wonder how few of the excellent
young men, well born and well educated,
who seek election at the hands of their con-
stituents, really know or care much about
the serious problems that vex the modern
soul. A young man of fortune and expecta-
tions takes a seat in the House of Commons
as he would a chair in Hyde Park, to pass
the time and gain a certain amount of

interest and amusement. He dallies with Bills that affect the well-being of thousands of citizens, or votes for or against an expedition of war that must cost the lives of hundreds of his fellow-men, with the agreeable insouciance and perfect self-possession that characterise a young gentleman sure of himself and dressed by a fashionable tailor. He votes because he has received a " whip," and he listens occasionally to a few speeches which bore him and give him a headache. To such the House of Commons is a lounge, a more or less eclectic club, a place associated rather with *ennui* than with duty, and yet a creditable place enough, and one that every man who has nothing to do, aspires to enter. In this light Dick himself had long regarded it, but, in spite of all, his friend Bruce's influence made itself felt as earnest convictions invariably must, and the superfluous vitality which had hitherto bubbled over in passion and flirtation was now devoted to understanding something of the difficulties and glories of statesmanship. He had not sought out Bruce lately for the reason that swayed most of his actions, because at this moment he did not need him. Every one was very friendly to him in the House, and the fact that for the first time the county had been won by a Liberal, and that Liberal a young man, redounded to his credit and gained him a certain amount of esteem among the older members. Besides which, Bruce's face reminded him of certain passages in his life which he was anxious to consign to oblivion :—his boyishly passionate adoration of Lady Fenchurch heightened by the hopelessness of the adoration ; his rapid cooling off the instant his beloved was in trouble, and by her trouble caused him annoyance and persecution ; his equally sudden engagement to Luce, and her inexplicable refusal to marry him, coupled with his latest shamefaced resolution to return to his allegiance to Lady Fenchurch, while hating the semi-humiliation it involved ;— these were causes sufficient to make any man avoid a friend cognisant of his variability and inclined to act the part of Mentor. Dick was certainly sobered. The events of the past year had not been without their effect : he no longer sought the society of racing-men or gamblers. He retired earlier to bed, except when kept up into the small hours by the exigencies of a division, and he seldom went to balls. He saw Lady Fenchurch occasionally; she was now restored to her usual health, and in her widow's weeds looked remarkably handsome. Miss Fenchurch, to whom everything had been confided, was their constant companion, and her absorption in the inevitable knitting made her a harmless and complaisant chaperon. The lovers had not much to say to one another; burnt-out love is difficult to relight, and Lady Fenchurch was usually occupied with her dress, while Dick, abstractedly smoking beside her, mused on the chances of the political future. They spent most of their time in the garden. Dick would run down for a day and remark the progress of the blossoms, or the brilliant aspect of the flower-beds, and these things afforded an item of conversation. It was very pleasant sitting under the big limes in an easy rocking-chair, with a profusion of cushions and rugs, and the sweet soft air, more sweet in contrast to the smoky, stifling atmosphere of London, and the hot oppressiveness of the House of Commons, played round his forehead and wafted across the scent of the neighbouring hayfield. If any one just a year before had foretold this scene, placid in its quiet, and perfect in its repose, Dick must have hailed the prospect with joy, and yet now in the society of this beautiful woman, soon to be his wife, he occasionally yawned, and fell into long spells of moody silence, which seemed a strange contradiction to the apparent blissfulness of his lot. Pleasant as was the beautiful solitude, the soothing hum of the bee, busily dipping into the bosoms of the honeyed flowers, the gentle rustling of the branches, or the far-off sounds of country life, he was invariably restless and anxious to get back to town, until one day Evelyn observed it and rallied him on his new love for work.

"Surely it is much nicer here than in town. You can't like hot dinners in stifling rooms and an atmosphere that seems to weigh like a stone on your head?"

"It is much pleasanter here," he said, leaning back with his arms behind his head, and sending up whiffs of pale smoke into the still air.

"Then what do you want? why are you so restless?"

She looked at him a little anxiously; no woman likes to feel that the power of her charms is waning. The Circes of real life never wish Ulysses to escape.

"Am I restless? perhaps it is the heat."

"But it is hotter in London. Would you like some iced drink? I will send up to the house at once."

"I am not a bit thirsty."

"Then," she said, a little wearily, "perhaps you have seen some one you like better than me? That Miss Denvil you told me you were riding with, who is she?"

"The daughter of a man I met in the House; a very nice little girl."

"And rich, I suppose? You don't want money now, Dick."

"No—thank goodness!"

"And this girl, what is she like?"

"I am sure I don't know. I can't describe her; she is like everyone else."

"Blue eyes, and golden hair, and a painfully small waist."

"Exactly; you have described her."

"I am sure I should not like her. Pushing

and forward too, I suppose; plays tennis
like a man, and smokes cigarettes after
dinner."

"Yes—don't you smoke?" he said lazily.

"How aggravating you are! You know
I never smoke."

"It is very unladylike, my dear," put
in Miss Fenchurch, who had dropped a stitch
in her knitting.

"I think I should like to go to London
for a day or two," said Evelyn, suddenly,
after a pause.

Dick looked surprised, and Miss Fenchurch
murmured :—

"No, my dear, really, should you?
Hadn't we better wait till the autumn?"

"Certainly not! I wish to go now. Have
you any objection?"

"No———" Dick looked a little puzzled
—"but isn't it rather hot?"

"I dare say I shall not mind. The truth
is you have infected me with your unrest,
and I feel I cannot stand another long dull
month in the country. I should lose my
appetite and get hipped."

"My dear, you should take a tonic, and
send for the doctor if you don't feel well."

"I am quite well, thank you; but you know it is the fashion of the present day. No one can stay long in the same place."

"I could live here for ever," said the old maid, casting a critical glance around.

Lady Fenchurch had her way, and a few days later was settled with her aunt in a private hotel. Dick took their rooms for them, and had them filled with flowers, at whose beauty Miss Fenchurch exclaimed with delight. Perhaps had she known that they were indebted for them to the taste of the valet, who had bought them in Covent Garden, she might not have been so touched at the attention.

"Very gallant of the young man," said Miss Fenchurch, sniffing at a rose, "very gallant. I must say he has most pleasing manners."

"Flowers are common enough in London," said her sister-in-law; "one can buy them round the corner, anywhere."

Evelyn had a shrewd suspicion that Dick had not given himself as much trouble as the old lady supposed.

"But the flowers are beautiful, just your

favourites, Evelyn, and many a man would not have thought of that."

Dick called in the evening and asked if the ladies were comfortable, and proposed the opera for the following night.

"The opera!" said Miss Fenchurch, "you forget we are in mourning; indeed, I really never could imagine why Evelyn so persistently wished to come to London, for of course we can go nowhere—a widow attracts so much attention."

"I will take a box, and Lady Fenchurch can sit behind the curtain."

"Oh, yes, I can sit behind the curtain, and I know so few people. There *can* be no objection," urged Evelyn.

So Miss Fenchurch was overruled, and the box at the opera was taken. Lady Fenchurch enjoyed music, and especially operatic music, and sat in her corner honestly delighted. One of her fine arms rested on the cushion of the box, and the other lay in her lap. Her handsome features were lit up by a pleased smile, and certainly Miss Fenchurch might have been excused for thinking she would attract attention, with her marble-white skin en-

hanced by the sable draperies and her large
eyes, whose lids drooped a little in languid
pleasure. Dick, to whom the opera was not
such a novelty, sat at the back of the box,
but occasionally leant forward to take a look
round the house, or to converse with Miss
Fenchurch, who asked innumerable questions
in ecstacies of astonishment and curiosity.
In one of the critical glances he thus threw
around, Dick thought he perceived some
familiar faces in the box opposite. They
were indeed Lady Eleanor with Luce, accompanied by a couple of young men. As Dick
leant foward he caught Luce's eyes fixed on
him with a pained expression. It was the first
time he had met her since their engagement,
with the exception of that one cursory
glimpse in the Park ; and he felt sorely
tempted to go round and speak to her. · But
an instant's reflection taught him that this
would be almost an insult. He could not go
to her straight from Lady Fenchurch's side,
and the fact of his being with a young lady
who remained carefully concealed behind a
curtain was in itself enough to raise her suspicions. How pale and sad she looked,
scarcely ever smiling, or seeming to care

what went on upon the stage, and only paying casual attention to the remarks of the
young man beside her. Dick wondered if
she had suffered. Perhaps the only real and
genuinely unselfish interest ever aroused in
him by a woman, Luce had evoked. He could
not help comparing her to other girls, and
remarking that the balance was entirely in her
favour. How he wished he could recall the
past, that Lady Fenchurch had been rich
and independent of him, so that he might
have married his little, gentle Luce, and
lived quietly with her in the country. He
could imagine what a tender, loving wife she
would have made, and that she would have
indulged in none of the caprices with which
other woman wearied him.

"What are you looking at so persistently?"
presently asked Lady Fenchurch, for the
curtain had fallen upon the second act, and
she was free to notice Dick's preoccupied
silence and abstracted gaze.

"Nothing—I mean it is a very full house;
how do you like the opera?"

"Very much; do you see a great many
people you know here to-night?"

"A few."

"I want to look too—there, I can just catch a bird's-eye view through the curtain; ah, now I see what attracted you so—Lady Eleanor Highview and her niece. Well, she *is* a plain girl."

She dropped the curtain, and resumed her former position. "Do you know, Dick, I think you are a dreadful flirt? I used to be jealous of your cousin Maud, and now I believe I ought to be jealous of that plain girl."

"That plain girl jilted me."

"Then your engagement to me is no great compliment, I am sure I am very much obliged." She put her bouquet up to her lips, and pretended to be annoyed.

"I should not have been free had she not jilted me."

"Didn't she care about you then?"

"I don't know."

"You *do* know, why do you try to deceive me?"

"Let us talk of something else. Does not my future life belong to you?"

"H'm! well, I suppose it does; and you don't wish me to ask inconvenient questions. It must be a bore to be taken up as Miss

Windermere was, in a moment of pique, and then dropped again a little later."

"I don't wish to discuss Miss Windermere."

" But she interests me; she is a study; she has good eyes; but she does not look lively; she would have been a dull companion to pass the rest of your days with."

"Miss Windermere is very clever."

"Oh! I suppose a kind of blue; reads Greek and goes in for the higher mathematics. Now, Dick, I am quite sure that is not at all in your line. You had far rather a woman were frivolous like me—confess I amuse you."

" Yes! but one cannot always expect to be amused."

" Dear me, I thought you men only lived for amusements, and left all the boring, tiresome things to us women. We always wear more rigid mourning and stay at home, while you dine out."

" What do you propose doing to-morrow?" said Dick, desirous to interrupt her flow of satirical talk. He could see Luce where he sat, and he fancied she had grown even paler.

" I must go to see the pictures and the

shops. I haven't been in London for such a long time, and there are quantities of things I am curious about."

"I should like to visit Kensal Green," said Miss Fenchurch, demurely; "I am told it is so beautifully kept."

"Oh! fancy being anxious to visit a churchyard; I hate to think of those things," said Evelyn, quickly.

"One ought always to think of one's latter end," replied Miss Fenchurch piously.

Dick hurried off the ladies a little before the end, in order to avoid the crush, but there had been some mistake about the carriage, and they were forced to wait a few moments in the hall. While thus engaged Lady Eleanor and her party swept down the stairs and confronted them.

There was no escape. Lady Eleanor bowed stiffly when she saw who was Dick's companion, and Luce gave him a piteous glance. Never, perhaps, had he felt himself in such a painful and constrained position. Lady Fenchurch appealed to him affectedly, as though to prove that he was without mistake her cavalier, and in a few moments they were once more alone.

" The deuce take women," thought Dick, angrily; "why do they want to come to London? If it had not been for this unlucky rencontre, no one would have suspected my relations with Evelyn Fenchurch, and now it will be all over London, and Luce must think I have shown indecent haste in thus braving public opinion."

CHAPTER X.

Luce seldom sang now. She had never been
a public performer; even in the smallest of
coteries, her timidity absolved her from all
necessity of giving her friends the more or
less appreciated pleasure of after-dinner
music, but she had loved to play and sing to
Granny, and in her moods of excitement
or depression she found relief in song. But
with the desire and the anticipation of
happiness her voice left her, and she fre-
quently sat dumb and silent before the key-
board, feeling unable to play a note, or to
lift her voice above a whisper. In certain
crises of emotion, music helps and comforts
us, and proves a kind of safety-valve, but
when we are crushed and miserable beyond
the power of endurance, the very sound of
music seems to irritate our pain. Neverthe-

less, the day after her vision of Dick at the
opera, she sat down to the piano in the
drawing-room, and feebly moved her hands
over the keys. She had not the power to
sing, but her fingers strayed almost without
sense of volition into a little piece of Bach's,
Granny was accustomed to play in the quiet
evenings at Long Leam. It began with a
quick gavotte in the minor mode, which
Granny executed with surprising delicacy
and precision, and contained a second movement, a kind of pastoral, of which Luce was
particularly fond. Leaning back as she
listened she could fancy the peasants dancing on the village green, and hear the
shepherd's pipe; an air of freshness and
candour seemed to surround and a flavour
of antiquated simplicity enchant her. The
music spoke of homely love, of simple truth
and constancy, and often as she heard the
familiar sounds they always produced on
her the same effect, that of pleasurable
content and quaint illusion. Now as her
fingers strayed she forgot for the moment
her weariness and her surroundings, and
saw again Granny sitting at the piano in
her prim upright pose, the pose habitual to

ladies of her time, dressed in her handsome
lilac brocade and pretty lace cap; her
mittened hands lightly moving over the
keys, and her kind head nodding in time to
the dance measure. Behind her was the
arched alcove with the brown-backed books
heaped together in tawny mustiness, and the
jars of priceless old china which garnished
the corners. The faded chintz covers of the
spindle-legged, uncomfortable chairs and
settees looked ghostly in the dim light, and
when Granny stopped playing there was a
hush of tangible silence around—the echoes
of the past alone haunted the room. Absorbed in a recollection which seemed so
clear and so real to her, Luce turned with a
start and a rude awakening from the dream
of the past she had delicately built up to a
sense of the present, when the door of the
drawing-room opened, and instead of the
old lady, and her music, and the shadows
and stillness of Long Leam, there presented
itself to her gaze the red satin furniture and
hot-house flowers of Lady Eleanor's drawing-room, and close beside her Bruce bowing,
hat in hand, and murmuring some confused

sentences, of which she scarcely gathered
the import.

"Ah, it is you, Mr. Bruce," she said,
regaining her composure by an effort;
"Lady Eleanor is out driving, and ——"

"And you were playing—do I disturb
you? Shall I go?"

"No, you can stay," she said indifferently, executing a rapid scale on the instru-
ment. "I daresay my aunt will soon return,
if you can wait."

"I can wait," said the young man, slowly
fidgeting a little nearer to Luce, who, without rising from the music-stool, had offered
him her hand. "The fact is, I am glad we
are alone; I wanted to talk to you quietly."

"One can never be quiet in London,"
said Luce, wearily; "there is such a perpetual whirl, and oh how sick one gets of it
all! those endless hot balls and tedious
parties, and the pretences and show which
all mean nothing. People inviting those
they don't care about, because it looks well,
and leaving out the old true friends who are
not smart or not fashionable enough to do
them honour."

"You would prefer to be at Highview?"

"Oh, yes, indeed." Luce rose and walked feverishly up and down. "Just think how beautiful the roses must be just now; that La France, with its grand pink blossom, and General Jacqueminot, with leaves like velvet, and an exquisite aroma, and the golden petals of the Rêve d'Or; you remember how luxuriously it grew over the trelliswork at the entrance to the rosary?"

"I remember you showed me the plant, but the roses were over when I first saw Highview."

"How glorious the summer in the country is; and to think that men's perverted tastes lead them to shut themselves up in a stifling town just when our English homes, and even this capricious English climate, are beautiful to perfection."

"Yes, it is strange. I know but little of the country, I have lived so much among my books; and yet I feel—Highview taught me to feel—its beneficial influence."

"You should come to us in the summer; but we shall scarcely be there this year till half the flowers are over," she added, with a sigh.

"Lady Eleanor wishes you to remain in

town ?" he asked, seating himself as he did so.

"Yes; she says it is a part of my education. I wish my education were finished."

"It is like college for young men—an initiation into life."

"Is this life ? It seems to me more like a kind of stupor of the mind, in which only a few of the senses are alive."

"You will no doubt emerge from the ordeal scatheless; the very fact that your heart is not in it will prevent any harm accruing to you. I should be very sorry if harm came to you." His voice shook slightly. Luce looked up surprised.

· "You need not be anxious," she said, quietly.

"But I am anxious," he answered quickly. "You are suffering, I am sure; just now, when I surprised you, there were tears in your eyes."

"I was thinking of Granny—of old Mrs. Carrol," she said, simply; "I miss her very much."

"Of course you do, Miss Windermere; it may seem strange, you may think me presumptuous; but you have been so much in my thoughts lately, if I could help you—if I —— ”

“ Thank you,” she said, gratefully ; “ the sympathy of a friend is always acceptable ; and we were friends at Highview, were we not ? ”

“ It has occurred to me,” he continued hastily, “ that I am answerable for your unhappiness, that it was through my persuasion that Dick Carrol became a candidate for West Thorpe, and consequently an inmate of your house; and that whatever annoyances befell you are owing to me.”

“ I have no annoyances,” she answered, rather coldly. He had no right on the score of kindness, to try and worm out her secrets.

“ Now I have offended you. I have little knowledge of society. I am ignorant of the terms in which I ought to express myself ; but, believe me, I would do anything, anything to serve you,” he said, earnestly.

“ I am sure of it.”

If she had doubted for one instant, the honest ring of Bruce’s voice would have reassured her. And the interest he showed her she knew was not scattered broadcast. He was reserved and shy, and as a rule avoided ladies' society. Consequently his attention was the more flattering, for in his own sphere of literature and study he was already well known and almost famous; she knew that also.

"When I see you sad it makes me miserable. Can I not help you—do you wish to see Dick?"

"No, no." She shook her head passionately.

"He has not behaved ill, surely. I pray of you confide in me—believe me —— "

"I have nothing to confide. Dick never behaved ill to me; we parted—because it was best so."

"And you are breaking your heart." He jumped up and restlessly moved about the room. "Is there nothing to be done? I am your slave, your knight, command me, use me."

"Indeed, Mr. Bruce, I need nothing. A girl must not sit down helplessly with her hands folded because she has not got just the bit of happiness she fancied—that would be weak and foolish. I try not to be weak."

"And is all your life to be passed thus?"

"No; I shall get better and stronger, and

perhaps I shall forget," she said, smiling through her tears. "I feel as if I could speak to you and treat you as my friend— as if you understood —— "

"Yes, I understand." And as he looked at the little fragile figure before him with the waxen complexion and the large eyes, that seemed with their brilliancy to efface the small oval face, he thought, "provided it does not kill her." The mental life was so great, the physical power so small.

"But there are moments when I feel as if I had been mistaken, as if I had presumptuously overruled the decrees of Providence, and sought to control fate with my own weak hands; and then I am devoured by tortures of remorse, of despair, and doubt."

"Trust yourself, trust your own instincts, they are right."

"Oh, you comfort me—it is something to be able to speak out without incurring blame or ridicule."

"Will you let me be your friend?—we are drawn together by a strange loneliness, you are alone, so am I, and we both feel the need of communion."

"But you are so clever, you have your

books; only yesterday I heard that your History had created a sensation."

"The critics have been kind, but, even if it had been different, their opinion would not have altered my convictions; where one writes only to please, one does no good work—it must grow solely from knowledge and love. My work has been everything to me hitherto."

"And now ——?"

"Now—I must not say it. I must not breathe it—you will be angry."

"Are we not to be friends? Why should I be angry?"

"Then I will tell you. Your image comes between me and my work ——"

"The image of your *friend*," she said, with emphasis, "should rather help than hinder work."

"But I dream, too—I dream of a time when that friend might be more to me. I think words that cannot be said, I fancy, I build castles, fairy castles, and sometimes I whisper to myself that I love ——"

Luce moved away a little, with a gesture of disapproval.

"Don't move; I may talk freely, mayn't

I? These are only dreams, you know, and dreams deceive; but I think, if I had the chance, how much I could love, and worship and *work* for the gentle object of my dreams."

"They are dreams, as you say, and they can never be fulfilled."

"Never? Oh, I know I am presumptuous, but as the humblest and most devoted of your servants, as the truest and most faithful of friends, as one who would count it honour to serve you, and a smile his highest reward—could you never permit me to love you thus?"

"Mr. Bruce," said Luce, very seriously, "all you have said is, no doubt, most flattering, and I daresay I am different to other girls; I ought to feel honoured by your preference, of which, indeed, I am not worthy; but it is my intention never to marry. I cannot marry without love—and I do not love—any one."

"Luce, you are trying to blind yourself. If you cannot let me be your slave, (I ask nothing, nothing in return) I will be content to wait and hope, if I may only be near you and hear your dear voice; but, if you will not allow my devotion, at least, do not kill yourself, do not ruin your whole life for a shadow. Let me go to Dick, he does not know how much you care, his heart is excellent, and let me tell him that you love him still."

"You must do nothing of the sort," she said, catching at his hand as he turned to go; "I do not wish for his love—now."

"You are sublimely unselfish, but you are foolish, too," he said, very sadly.

"Perhaps—are not all women foolish?—but yet they know their own heart best."

"Ah yes, who could attempt to read a woman's heart? Not I for one."

"You will forget all that has passed between us to-day, will you not, Mr. Bruce? Don't think any more of me; I shall be quite happy, or, if you must think of me, remember I am content; but plunge as before into study and research—some day you will be famous, and I shall be *so* glad!"

"And I shall have lost you. Oh, Luce, my perfect Luce, let me try and make you happy, I know so well all you want; trample on me, despise me—do what you like—but let me love you."

"Just now I told you that my heart was

dead, that I can never, never love again," she said, with gentle reproof; his earnestness raised her tender pity even while it wearied her.

"I know you said so, but all life cannot pass thus."

"Perhaps life will not be long for me; at any rate, its duration is not in our own hands."

"If I had only met you first would you have loved me then? you look so fragile, and yet you are so tenaciously strong in your affections."

"I am tired," she said, leaning her head back against the chair; "is not the heat oppressive?"

"And I have tired you, you, to whom I would fain spare the smallest fatigue; how selfish I am! Luce—I am still your friend, am I not? you will not retract your word, you will tell me all that concerns you, you will keep back nothing—it will be all I shall have to live for now," he added, sadly.

"And your book?"

"My book of course, but nothing, nothing can take your place." He walked absently towards the door, then, remembering he had not said farewell, he hurried back to where Luce sat pale and motionless in her chair, took one of her small white hands, kissed it passionately, stroking and kissing it with the broken words a mother uses over her child. Then, suddenly, without stopping to see if his passion had moved her, he turned and left the room. The whole thing had been so sudden, such a surprise, that Luce sat on for some moments where he had left her, stunned, the touch of his kisses seeming to burn her hand. The passion of love in cold, self-centred men is sometimes terrible in its intensity when once the outer chilly crust is pierced.

"Poor fellow!" she thought, moaning to herself. "Poor fellow, if I could only have loved him; if I could but have made him happy; but I can never forget Dick. His memory seems to have dried up every other emotion within me. Ah, if I could—if I could ——"

CHAPTER XI.

Bruce walked straight home after leaving
Lady Eleanor's house. The distance was
long, and the heat intense; but he felt
neither heat nor fatigue. He passed through
the little garden with a listless step, noticing
neither the scarlet peonies forming so bright
a bit of colour, nor the carnations Mrs.
Flinks had spent all the afternoon in tying
up carefully. He went straight upstairs to
the little sitting-room, in which we have
already seen him so often, sat down beside
the table on which the big folios were
heaped, laid his arms on the table and his
head on his arms, and sobbed, sobbed, for the
first time since he left school, like a child.
He had been a poor weak fool. What need
had he to insult her with his love, when he
only meant to show his sympathy, and to

comfort her? If it had been conic sections
now, or the early life of the Anglo-Saxons,
he would have known how to speak; he
could have conversed rationally; but love—
what did he know of love or girls? Ah! he
was an egregious ass, and it served him all
well right.

Meanwhile this summer's day evidently
encouraged inflammatory tendencies. Mrs.
Flinks was shelling peas in the back kitchen,
and as she did so talking to Eves.

"Yes, you may laugh, but I'm tired of
this desolate life; that affair with the young
lawyer came to nothing; he wouldn't propose till he knew the amount of my fortune,
and I was too sly for him; I wasn't going to
let my gentleman have everything so easy
as that."

"I am sure you're right comfortable
here," said Eves, with arms as usual immersed in a tub of hot water up to the
elbows. "There's that Mr. Bruce, he gives
no trouble at all, and pays his rent as
regular as clockwork."

"Yes," sighed the widow, dropping the
peas into the basin with a resigned tic-tac.

" I used to think he was a fish. now I think he's a calf, tormented by calf-love."

" Lor, Mum, and whatever put that into your head ? "

" Well, he goes out more, and he's getting particular about his dress. His coat really looks as if it were made by a tailor instead of by some old woman who had cut it out of a spare piece of alpaca, and sewed it together again at the seams."

" Well, I never, you do surprise me," said Eves, making a perfect blanc-mange of soap-suds, for it was washing-day, and she was " getting up " a few little things for her mistress.

" It's simmering, Eves; I'm sure it's simmering."

" What, Mum, the saucepan? It's all right."

" No, that man's love; he's beginning to feel—is more wide-awake now; he looks at me as he goes out as if I were a human being, and not a tortoise; once even, when I shook my cap-ribbons in his face pretending to stoop down and unlock the door, he took an end of the ribbon in his hand, and as he stood there said quite sheepish-like, "What a pretty colour! do you call this pink?"

"You don't say so," said Eves, not even interrupting her splashing to show surprise.

"Now you know, Eves, a quiet husband would suit me in many ways: firstly, because men are more constant when they don't see much company, and then they're more economical, and besides they're always to your hand if you want them."

"Surely, Mum, he ain't proposed yet?"

"No; it's easy to see he's a gentleman; he's always so polite, though shy in his manner, and—Eves, it's Leap Year!"

"Why, Mum, you're never going to propose to him?"

"Hold your tongue, you silly old woman; there's more ways than one of proposing. You can wheedle and coax a man into most things."

"Well, I declare; I should like my husband to propose to me, and not feel I had to do the man's work for him."

"Eves, an idea has struck me. Here, take this basin, I'm going upstairs to change my gown, and I want you to help me ——"

Eves did as she was bid, and drew her

long red arms out of the soapsuds regretfully.

"Such a beautiful lather as it was, too," she said, as she followed ner mistress upstairs.

A quarter of an hour later Mrs. Flinks knocked at Bruce's door.

"Come in," he said, quietly, for even when disturbed he was patient.

The landlady walked in; she was nicely dressed in a fashionably-made summer dress, and wore a new and bewitching cap.

"Ah! you are alone, Mr. Bruce, and dear me, those Venetian blinds not drawn down; how careless of Eves! I must give her a good scolding." She looked coquettishly over her shoulder as she proceeded to unfasten the blinds.

"Pray do not scold her," he said, without moving, apparently engrossed in a folio, "I opened them myself."

"Then shall I do them up again?" she asked, letting them fall with a bang.

"No, no; you can leave them, the sun is nearly down."

"To be sure it is."

Mrs. Flinks pulled up the blinds, and,

despairing of attracting her lodger's attention otherwise, came back and stood beside him.

"And to think you're always poring over those big books. You're looking pale, Mr. Bruce; it isn't good to work in this hot weather; you should take a rest."

He shook his head. "I can't afford the time."

"Stuff! why one volume of that history is out, and I'm sure it's stodgy enough to satisfy the public for a bit."

"I am afraid you are not an admirer of my works, Mrs. Flinks."

"Indeed, sir, I am; I learnt history and geography and the use of the globes at school, but I don't think we had quite such fat books to read out of. You'll excuse me, sir, but this weather is a little trying."

Herewith the widow drew a chair to the table, and Bruce, who could not bear to be rude to the humblest woman, was forced to endure her proximity. She looked round the room.

"Aren't you dull here sometimes all alone? You don't go out as much as some gentlemen."

" I cannot work except alone."

" And do you never *play?*" she asked, with a seductive roll of her eye.

" I am afraid I am uncomfortably serious."

" No, no, not uncomfortable, not at all. For my part, I prefer a man with some stamina."

" Indeed."

Bruce hoped she would soon come to the point to which she was leading up, and then depart; he fancied, perhaps, she had come to consult him on some money trouble, or about an investment.

" I don't think that friend of yours, Mr. Dick, has any stamina ; he's too fond of throwing about shillings and half-crowns to hansom cabmen."

" He is rich, and I am not."

" Well, riches are not *everything*, though of course they do count for a great deal. I have some little savings of my own, too; it's right to save, don't you think, Mr. Bruce ? "

" Certainly."

" And whoever married me need not take me quite penniless."

" Are you thinking of marrying then, Mrs. Flinks?"

" It is lonely, sir, for a widow—very lonely—and the heart feels its own solitude."

" It is not good for man to be alone," said Bruce, under his breath. " I suppose that applies even more to women."

" Of course, sir, and you, too, must be lonely."

Bruce made a deprecatory movement.

" Not but what marriage is a lottery, only when people are quiet and orderly and know their own mind there is some security. It's a great thing, too, for a man to have a profession, and a decent one. I suppose writing is a very nice profession, brings you in a good deal and doesn't require much outlay, no plant or machinery, or offices, and no regular hours necessary."

" Well, I should scarcely call literature a paying concern, and it certainly means a great deal of work," said Bruce, with a smile.

" Indeed!" Mrs. Flinks looked a little disappointed. " But you only want pen, ink, and paper, and a table. People must be very poor indeed, when they haven't got that."

"You have forgotten two other requisites, brains and perseverance."

"Brains—of course, you must be intelligent, but, then, every business requires brains; you wouldn't believe how wearing it is to be a landlady; and perseverance— where should I be if I didn't drudge away day after day?"

"And you succeed, too, Mrs. Flinks—you say you have saved money."

"A little, a very little, but it's uphill work." She leant her arms on the table, and pulled out her pocket handkerchief with a flourish and a considerable amount of sniffling.

"Are you in trouble, Mrs. Flinks?" asked Bruce, fairly puzzled at the widow's manœuvres.

"No, sir, not exactly, but —— " here she sniffed again, "I want a friend; what is a poor weak woman without a friend? May I take your hand—it is easier to speak so, and if you— can't you guess, sir, what I feel?—brought up as I was to better things, and now reduced to let lodgings—ah sir, you're a man, you must have a heart."

"No, no!" exclaimed Bruce, drawing away his hand, "I have no heart." He thought that at last he guessed her meaning; he noticed with alarm the new cap, the diamond ring, her best, a Cape diamond set in massive gold, she wore on her finger; her appeal to his heart. No, no: was this, indeed, the satire on his sentimentality of the afternoon? He was being paid out in his own coin, and the very thought of it disgusted him. Mrs. Flinks sobbed more gently. Her ample bosom heaved in slow and decreasing movement under her summer dress. She clutched at her pocket-handkerchief nervously, and leant towards Bruce, as if she expected him to offer her his shoulder for support. In such an attitude, an attitude that a genteel young man would gladly avail himself of when in company with a nice-looking woman, it would have been easy to murmur endearing words, which need not be very coherent or very grammatical, but which would serve their purpose and clench the affair. Presently, like drops of cold water falling on a heated surface, she heard

Bruce's voice saying, in a suspiciously frigid tone,

" I am afraid you are not well, my dear madam—shall I call Eves ? "

" Oh dear, no," the widow quickly withdrew her handkerchief from her face, " I am quite well, but a little flustered; I'm of a nervous temperament. Dear pa always used to say it was the sign of a most refined and delicate organisation—dear papa loved refinement, although he was a ship's captain, and—dear me, Mr. Bruce, where are you going ? "

" To fetch you a glass of cold water, madam."

" Oh, pray, pray don't leave the room, I cannot stand solitude, often I wish—I wish you would let me come and sit beside you in the evening. I could bring my work and sit as still as a ghost, even the scratching of your pen is better than nothing—and then I could make you some tea—I have some my late husband gave me, it cost twenty shillings a pound, and it has a wonderful flavour —— "

" Why, Mrs. Flinks, what would people say if you came and sat in my room."

"I don't care what people say," she cried, throwing him a suggestive flash from her dark eyes; "but," dropping her eyes again, "I should be very happy."

Bruce stood aghast. He could not put the woman out by the shoulders, and how could he persuade her to leave the room? "My good woman —— "

"Don't good woman me; listen, Mr. Bruce, I'm young, and I'm considered good-looking, and I'm saving, as I've told you, and it's Leap Year—now, will you take me?"

"Take you?"

"Don't you understand—bless the man where are his wits?—will you have me for your wedded wife, to have and to hold? I'll mend your socks, and look after your clothes, and sit quiet when you're busy, and keep the inkstand filled—and we shall neither of us feel lonely — eh, what do you say — wouldn't it be a nice thing for both of us?"

"A very nice thing, no doubt, but entirely out of the question."

"Why, pray why," she said, waxing angry and red in the face, "ain't my house good enough for you, when you ink every blessed bit of furniture you come across, and

I—with a piano and prints in my sitting-room, and a green moreen sofa, as good as new—and don't think I'm uneducated, I was in Paris and learnt French and went to the Louvre, and know how to put on a bonnet with the best of 'em, mincing, short-sighted, painted madams—out of the question, indeed!"

"Listen, Mrs. Flinks," said Bruce, in his gravest manner, "it is always a mistake when people try to reverse their proper positions. You are my landlady, I am your lodger—do not let us alter circumstances. I have been very comfortable here, and I think you have no fault to find with me; allow matters to remain just as they are, and I promise you never to revert to this little episode again."

Mrs. Flinks sat dumb with rage and disappointment. Presently she said with a pout, "I don't think you *are* a gentleman; at least—are you engaged?"

"No, indeed, I assure you I am not."

"Then you are *not* a gentleman, to lead a poor woman on to show the state of her heart and her feelings, and to expose her weakness, and then turn round on her like a steel spring, and say, 'Shut up, you're only my landlady.'"

"I don't think I spoke quite so rudely as that."

"I daresay you wrapped it up a bit more in your long words, and your fine language, but the upshot was the same, it meant, 'You be off and don't trouble me any more.'"

"Well, we will not dispute," he went up to the fire-place, where reigned a cascade of coloured shavings of paper, supposed to add beauty to the blackness of the grate, and leant against the mantel-piece, over which hung a fly-blown glass, "but don't you think perhaps I am right, and that my advice was good?"

"I think you're a ——" she stopped, choking with anger in search of an epithet "a mean scribbler—a fish—there ——"

He stood calmly, a sad smile flickering over his countenance. There was an irony about the persistency and impotent wrath of this woman that reminded him of his own hopeless love. After all, allowing for the difference of satin chairs and hot-house flowers, and greasy reps, and second-rate prints, and cheap muslin curtains, human nature was

the same in both cases. Moths singeing
their wings in the flames, aspiring to a distant and unattainable star. He could not
hard or cruel to the poor little woman; the
pity for her was mixed with his own self-
contempt. He, the strong wise man who
had dipped deep into the well of philosophy,
and drank of the cup of learning, had been
foolish and blind, and this silly creature in
her finery, and with her meretricious charms,
was no worse.

He spoke kindly, "Mrs. Flinks, let us be
friends; I am very sorry if I misunderstood
you—if as you say I led you on—you must
forgive a student who is not versed in the
ways of the world."

"You're knowing enough," she muttered,
"to get yourself out of a scrape any how.
You're not so soft as I thought; perhaps
after all you're a good riddance."

"If it comforts you to think so I shall not
be angry, but believe me I should not like
to hurt any woman's feelings."

"A lady, sir, I'm a lady, though I do let
lodgings. Woman's feelings indeed! I
suppose you think you're speaking to your
washerwoman?"

"I beg your pardon, Mrs. Flinks, I scarcely know how to speak."

"Well, I think you've spoken enough. There, I'm going, I've passed as unpleasant an afternoon as ever I passed in my life. I only hope when you propose to a young lady she'll treat you as you've treated me —woman indeed, I declare!"

Therewith Mrs. Flinks gathered herself up, shook her capstrings and her bangles warningly in Bruce's face as he held open the door for her to pass out, and in a storm of frowns, pouts, angry glances and flashes from the brilliant black eyes, departed.

"Well I never, Eves," she said, as she sailed into the kitchen in all her finery, "Bruce *is* a fish after all."

"What has he done now, mum?"

"Done? don't ask me, don't speak of him, and Eves—I feel so faint. I should like a relish with my tea; could you, could you get me some nice fresh shrimps?"

CHAPTER XII.

IMMEDIATELY after the unpleasant meeting at the theatre Dick urged Lady Fenchurch to return home. She had visited the Academy, he argued, and seen all the exhibitions, and been to the opera, and now it was time to leave London. With much regret Evelyn yielded to his entreaties; she had never passed more than a few days in London, and it seemed to her that in the bustle and whirl of the gay city lay unknown possibilities of new excitement. However, Miss Fenchurch supported Dick's urgent entreaties and Evelyn allowed herself to be overruled. When they reached Oakdene the country was looking its loveliest. The green of the spreading trees still retained its tender and delicate hue, the cottage gardens formed a blaze of pure white lilies, roses, and climbing honeysuckle, each hedge was a thing of beauty crowned with trailing wreaths of clematis and winding tendrils of convolvulus. As the carriage turned from the dusty road into the lodge-gates, and drove up the shady avenue, Evelyn herself heaved a breath of relief to be once more in the cool sweet air.

"It is a very pretty place," Dick said reflectively, looking round at the park.

"I wonder if its next owner will appreciate it as he should, it is only mine for a year, you know," said Miss Fenchurch, with a sigh.

"Is the man young?" asked Evelyn.

"I don't know, I am sure. I think not. A middle-aged man with a family, I believe, but such a distant cousin, we have no interest in him."

Lady Fenchurch was silent. A middle-aged man with a family sounded hopeless. If it had been different, if he had been free and young, well, she was only marrying Dick as a kind of provision for her future. She could not live poor and friendless after having been mistress of Oakdene. She stole a look at Dick. His brow was seamed by lines she had never before noticed; he looked worried and certainly older; he was gentle to her, anxious for her welfare, but she could not conceal from herself that sometimes he seemed bored and sad.

"Here we are," said Miss Fenchurch, joyfully, "and there is Puggy, and what fine flowers the gardener has brought!—how do you do, Biggs, and Mrs. Holden?" this to the butler and housekeeper, who waited respectfully on the stone steps to receive them, while the gardener, redfaced and hatless, stood by the pedestal vases holding a large bouquet of hothouse flowers in his hand. Miss Fenchurch was honestly pleased to be home again; she was like a mushroom grown in a meadow, she could take root nowhere but at home, and the acute pang it caused her even to think of the time when she must leave Oakdene to the tender mercies of a new owner, would scarcely have been guessed from her usually sedate and indifferent manner.

Lady Fenchurch stepped leisurely out of the carriage (she was not so *very* glad to be home), and the servants received Dick with the implied courtesy and respect due to one

who was the future husband of their lady.
Servants are quick at surmises, and they had
long ago guessed the relations in which
Dick and Evelyn stood to each other. In
the library was a table with the tea-tray
upon it, and a goodly pile of crimson strawberries set among green leaves heaped on a
dish. Lady Fenchurch began to nibble at
them directly, plunging her white fingers
into the rosy mass. Miss Fenchurch attacked
a bundle of letters and business communications, and Dick went to the window and
looked out. Before him stretched the lawn
and the flower-beds, one brilliant sheet of
colour, but he was not thinking of them, his
mind had conjured up a vision which
annoyed while it pursued him. He saw
always Luce's pale face, her sad eyes fixed
upon him with a kind of reproof and
entreaty. She was certainly paler and
thinner. Perhaps the season had not agreed
with her, late hours were trying to some
girls. After all everything was her own
doing, he had been ready to marry her, to
fulfil the contract, and *she* had willed it
otherwise. Well, nothing could be changed
now, he must not desert Evelyn. He turned

and saw her standing there, smiling and beautiful, happy with her strawberries. Little things satisfied her; she at least was never likely to break her heart.

"Have you as good strawberries as these at Long Leam?" she asked, noticing his stedfast gaze.

"Yes, I believe so."

"You tell me so little," she said, reproachfully, as she daintily wiped the red stains from her fingers. "Are there many greenhouses, and do you grow orchids? I don't care for orchids, they cost a great deal, and they make very little show."

"No, there are no orchids."

"Your grandmother was very fond of flowers," said Miss Fenchurch, looking up from her letters. "I remember she gained prizes, several times, at the county flower-show."

"You never half describe the place, and you know I have not been there," said Evelyn.

"Well, would you like to see it?"

"Of course I should, if it is to be my future home."

"I think it would be very pleasant to

drive over there in this nice fine weather," added Miss Fenchurch; "there could be no risk of catching cold, and we could take luncheon with us."

"I dare say I could find you something to eat," he said laughing; "Long Leam is not in the desert."

"Is any one living there, then?" said Evelyn, who had thrown herself into an easy-chair.

"Yes, my uncle and aunt Vincent."

"Those horrid people!" burst out Evelyn.

"I let them stay there for a little—they are not rich, you know."

"And very grasping of course, I have heard all about them. I must say you are very forgiving."

Dick coloured. It was not generosity, but a kind of indifferent carelessness, that prompted him to offer his relations hospitality. He suddenly remembered Mrs. Vincent's extraordinary letters, and her attempts to worm herself into his confidence, and felt that his generosity must appear pure folly.

"When will you go?" he asked abruptly.

"Oh directly, any day," said Evelyn who was gradually recovering her spirits, in any-

thing but widow-like fashion. Miss Fenchurch was thoughtful. "Perhaps your
uncle and aunt will not like it."

"They are only lodgers, only there on
sufferance," laughed Evelyn, forgetting the
similar situation she occupied at Oakdene, "they must go out some time or
other."

"I can write, and tell them I am coming,
and shall bring some friends," said Dick. "I
ought to go there really, for I have so much
business."

"You must arrange it as you like," said
Miss Fenchurch, bustling off to order the
dinner. Dick and Evelyn were left alone.
They were not often alone, for Miss Fenchurch understood the duties of chaperone
very literally, and, having due regard to the
exigencies of mourning, Dick never ventured
to ask any of the privileges of a lover. He
touched her hand night and morning, he
called her Evelyn, and he looked as much as
he dared at her creamy skin and the depths
of her fine dark eyes. But the prospect of
matrimony, certainly, seemed to cool his
ardour. The speeches he had poured out
to Evelyn Bray as freely as the fountain

lavishes its spray he never made to Evelyn Fenchurch. It was true that she never encouraged him; she seemed perfectly happy to have him near her, to call upon him for all the little offices a man can render, to ask his advice, and to enjoy the comforts of her easy life, but she never indulged in the sweet unreasoning talk that makes the bliss of lovers, in the delicious teazing quarrels, and inexpressibly delightful makings-up, that constitute the historical behaviour of two persons about to be married. There was friendship between them, a kind of cool gratitude on her side, a kind of disillusioned duty on his. Something of this sort passed through his mind as he saw her nestled in one of her peculiarly graceful postures in the depths of the arm-chair, one white hand negligently hanging over the arm, and her two little feet crossed on the small stool before her. The pose was suggestive, full of beauty and passive sensuousness.

"Evelyn!" She slightly turned her head.

"Shall you like going to see my house, your home that is to be?"

"Oh yes," she said, "it won't be a very

hot long drive, will it? Rachel fidgets me
so with her knitting when I am in the carriage."

"I used not to think it long when I rode
over to see you last year—do you remember
that day in the pine-wood, when you were so
unhappy."

"Oh please don't talk of disagreeable by-
gones. I can't think why one is never
allowed to forget."

"Oh! if one only could!" he said with an
accent of intense earnestness.

"Of course one can. Try not to think
of disagreeable things."

"Do you never think?"

The speech was almost rude but he felt he
must utter it.

"Never more than I can help. What is
the use? Nobody can alter fate."

"I am not a fatalist. I think if I had
known—oh, yes—things might have been
different even for me."

"But then you would *not* have known,"
she said, placidly twisting her rings on her
slim fingers. "That is the beauty of not
worrying oneself; one never knows what

may happen, and all the precautions one takes in case of accidents are useless."

" Do you love me, Evelyn ? " he asked, gravely.

"I? Of course; I thought we settled all that long ago."

" Settled it ! Do you mean ended it ? "

" No ; you will perversely misunderstand. Are we not engaged ? Well, is not that settled."

" I was engaged to another girl once."

" Oh, yes, I know, that plain Luce ; but you broke it off ; you were quite right. You had no need to marry for money."

" I was not marrying her for money. Perhaps it may seem strange to you, that girl loved me."

" Really ! Then I wonder she let you go. I shouldn't, I know."

" Luce is a strange girl, but she is very highminded."

" Please don't talk to me of the perfections of the girl you didn't marry ; that would be nearly as bad as a discourse on the virtues of a departed wife ; the best proof of her unsuitability is that you did not marry her."

" And you don't believe in self-sacrifice ?"

" Self-sacrifice! a thing for old maids and sisters of charity. I don't believe any girl gives up her lover from a sense of duty; that sort of duty merely implies a very poor kind of love." Evelyn spoke with assurance, a half contemptuous smile playing round her lips.

Dick, who had worked himself up into a kind of belief that Luce was almost a heroine, a self-sacrificing, loving girl, now decided that he must have been mistaken; women surely judged their own sex more accurately than men could do, and Luce might not have cared for him. He felt a little happier, and at the same time strangely disappointed. He would have liked Luce to be miserable because she had lost him; and he would have liked Evelyn to be proud of her own triumph. Instead of which she took it all as a matter of course, and he seemed to have been tossed from one woman to the other like a kind of shuttlecock.

" When shall we go to Long Leam ?" he began again.

" Pray arrange it with Rachel. She will

know all about the sandwiches, and the horses, and the distance."

" But I want *you* to care," he said, trying to infuse tenderness into his voice.

" So I shall, if the place is as nice as you say, and there are plenty of greenhouses. I am passionately fond of fruit."

" That is it!" he said to himself, as he went upstairs to dress for dinner. " Passionately fond of *fruit*, but not of *me*. Have I made a mistake after all, and been ridiculously Quixotic?" And again the image of Luce pursued him in his dreams, and he heard her say in that soft liquid voice, which always soothed him,

" Do you think I can make you happy? I will try, but *do* you think I can?"

Her diffidence was very charming, for when did a young man think himself unworthy to possess the prize for which his soul thirsted?

CHAPTER XIII.

THE warm and luscious July weather continued. The expedition to Long Leam was accomplished under the most favourable auspices, and Mrs. Vincent, fortunately ignorant of her nephew's engagement, received Lady Fenchurch with acid politeness. At all times she was jealous of the influence of pretty women, and especially so of the woman who had already entrapped Dick into her toils. But she remembered her own precarious position, and, like many of her betters, swallowed the indignity of condescension for the advantages to be gained therefrom.

"What a quaint old house!" observed Evelyn, looking round the drawing-room wonderingly. "And what old-fashioned furniture!"

"My grandmother took care of all the old things, and never bought any new. Poor thing! I remember well, she said my wife would want new furniture, and she would save her money for the purpose."

"Very nice of her, indeed," said Evelyn, poking her fingers into jars full of *pot-pourri*, and feeling the thin old damask of the curtains; "of course one couldn't live without comfortable chairs and dozens of little tables. I wonder how those old people managed."

"They managed very well," said Dick, a little drily, piqued at the contempt that pierced through her condescending praises. "I am sure Granny was a picture."

"That's so like men; they never know what one has on, and because an old lady wears a handsome silk gown they think her beautifully dressed. Now, pale lilac silks are quite out of fashion."

"Oh, I don't know," he said, biting his moustache impatiently; "I can't quite talk about Granny unconcernedly. She was so good to me. But come now and have a look at the bedrooms; there is a lovely one that faces the west—see if you would like that."

" Not the one your grandmother died in," said Evelyn quickly, with a shudder. " I am *so* afraid of ghosts."

" No, not that one," he said, contemptuously; "one in the newer wing." She followed him, shaking her handsome crape-laden skirts as she went.

Mrs. Vincent noticed everything, and an expression of ill-will passed over her countenance.

" Those two are a little too fond of each other's company," she said, with an unpleasant look at Miss Fenchurch. The old maid was her match.

" Those two ? Ah, you mean Evelyn and Mr. Carrol. Poor child! her nerves have been so badly shaken ever since my poor brother's death, that I am glad if she will take the smallest interest in anything."

" She looks well nourished," remarked Mrs. Vincent, with a genteelly modulated snort.

" Appearances are deceptive," said the old maid, pulling her knitting out of her pocket.

" You only knit," said Mrs. Vincent,

dropping the obnoxious subject; "you should see my girl's crewel-work."

"Crewel-work, fudge!" replied Miss Fenchurch. "Now, there's some sense in knitting; hand-made stockings have twice the wear in them, but I can't see the use of covering sofas and chairs with things that look like darned dusters—darned, too, with worsted that don't match."

Mrs. Vincent shrugged her shoulders, so much plain good sense shocked her. Had she not spent mints of money in procuring for her daughters all the advantages of fashionable accomplishments?

Meanwhile the young people, tired of rambling, had come to a stand-still in the large best bedroom. The western setting sun threw slanting beams of rosy light upon the carpet and on their faces, and touched Evelyn's finger-tips with a pretty ruddiness.

"Confess it's a nice old house," said the young man, looking round with a proud sense of possession, "and it's so well built— such thick walls, such doors, see; and the paneling—those old fellows did know how to build."

"Yes," she said, fascinated by the quaint

curves of the old carved chimney-piece, "the walls are as thick as those of a prison."

"What a comparison! it shall never be a prison to you."

"No," she answered, laughing, and moving on to examine a print. "I can admire this at least—what a sweet Bartolozzi!"

After luncheon they visited the gardens, and paced the smooth gravel-walks, and went through the grove, which, damp with a layer of decaying leaves in the autumn, now offered to their feet the softest carpet of green moss. Lady Fenchurch was in great spirits. She laughed at Dick's little sentimentalities over the place; suggested an improvement here or an alteration there, and viewed everything with the eye of an expert. Dick would have liked her to be a little more sober, a little more subdued, but how is it possible, except in a carping spirit, to find fault with a beautiful woman who leans on your arm as she walks, and accentuates her observation by the slightest possible pressure whenever she is interested. Evelyn passed a pleasant day, and Dick tried to feel perfectly satisfied. Miss Fenchurch spent a less happy day, for Mrs. Vincent annoyed her, and showed her nothing really interesting except a new kind of incubator warranted to hatch chickens by the thousand. The sight of this arrested Miss Fenchurch's attention for a considerable time; she wanted to know how everything was managed, and whether the machinery ever went out of order, and the exact principle of its working, and how the heat was to be regulated. Occupied in these housewifely cares the latter part of the afternoon passed more quickly than she had anticipated. Dick watched the ladies drive off with mixed feelings. He had stayed behind on a plea of business, and he rather dreaded facing aunt Vincent in the bosom of her family. He was certain she would ask disagreeable questions, and show interfering inquisitiveness. But to his surprise she did nothing of the kind. She talked of indifferent subjects, carved the lamb, and dispensed the strawberries with affability if not with grace, while Vincent himself was in an affectionate state of semi-sobriety, and Dolly and Eliza, as usual, giggled innocently together at nothing. Dick alleged

heavy arrears of letter-writing as an excuse
for not reappearing in the drawing-room
after dinner, and retired to his own den with
a pipe to chew the cud of solitary fancy.
He missed his grandmother more than he
could have believed, and now that he had
attained the wishes of his heart, now that
he was rich, courted, and free to marry the
woman for whom he had once conceived a
kind of insane passion, he felt a strange
sense of emptiness and dissatisfaction. He
filled his pipe and sat motionless, thinking
and smoking, the pile of letters lying untouched before him. He reviewed his past,
and remembered what he had so often
said to Bruce, "all I ask is to be allowed to
live my own life as I please."

Faithful Bruce, where was he now ?
Plunged as usual in study he supposed ; *he*
could find happiness in that, while Dick
with every desire gratified still wished and
longed for—he knew not what. He resolved
to write to Bruce ; he was to blame in not
having done so sooner, for the poor student
had no time to make new friends, and naturally clung to the old ones. This sultry
summer weather too, though cool under the

wide-spreading old trees of Long Leam,
must be stifling in London. Bruce might
be ill, knocked up by work and heat. Why
should he not come here and set up his inkstand and folios in one of the many cool
chambers of the semi-inhabited old house?
He might work undisturbed. Dick did not
care, for he could roam about the fields and
look at the young pheasants and break in
the chestnut colt. Certainly Bruce must
come and see Dick at home, in his own
house, master of his property, doing as he
listed. He took up his pen to write the
letter while he was in the mind, and as he
did so the clock struck two. Two o'clock
already, and how still the old house seemed.
His den panelled with old oak was dark at
all times, and now only dimly illuminated
by the light of two wax-candles placed on
the writing-table. A crowd of shadows
seemed to gather round, and a number of
old memories crept about him. How many
people had sat in that room already, and
thought their thoughts, and fretted out their
passions, who now lay mouldering in the
dust. Sometimes in an old house, filled with
the memories of long years, the ghosts of

bygone ancestors seem to be more real than
one's own petty life. Dick felt it at that
moment. He laid his pipe on the table and
buried his face in his hands. That life he
had wanted to live for himself, was it indeed
his own, was it not rather the accumulated
sum of all those ghostly ancestors' lives ?
The family traits, the family weaknesses,
had they not always hemmed him round and
carried him away. The long line of fore-
fathers counted for something after all ; the
massive walls had retained some germ of
spiritual affinity ; the very air was impreg-
nated with the odour of their dead bones.
Live his own life, who could do it ? *noblesse
oblige* in the strongest sense by hereditary
tendencies. He sighed. The atmosphere
seemed stifling, like the heaviness that is
the predecessor of a thunderstorm. That
odour too, that filled his nostrils, how strange
it was, like something sulphurous. No doubt
the lateness of the hour, the gloomy shadows
around, made him fancy all these queer se-
pulchral visions ; yet certainly there was
something abnormal in the night. An over-
powering dense heat, a smokiness in the
air. A tiny rim of light stole under the

door at that instant. Half stupidly he wondered if it were uncle Vincent going to bed, then with a sudden return of calm reason he guessed instinctively at the cause of his odd sensations. He started up, taking the candle in his hand, and threw the door open sharply. A thick cloud of smoke burst in through the aperture, almost stifling him, and a red spot in the distance confirmed his fears. Down the dark passage he flew, pushed open the swing-door that led into the gallery, where one peaceful night before among the moonbeams and the silence he held Luce for the first time in his arms, and heard her broken words of love. No time for memories now. The oaken floor was cracking, flames darting up to the ceiling. He turned and flew back down the passage, stopping only to peal the loud alarm-bell, and hurried by to knock at his aunt's door crying " fire ! fire ! " then darted hither and thither, calling, waking, terrifying the inmates of the house, until the servants, trembling and half awake in their scantily hustled on garments, stood round him.

Dick was in his element. He was brave, and he knew how to command. The buckets, some of which were already mouldy from age and disuse, were quickly brought out, a cordon formed to the pump in the stable-yard, and several messengers dispatched for aid and a fire-engine to West Thorpe. The stupified servants worked with a will, and presently Mrs. Vincent and the girls, white with fear, joined the salvage party. But the age of the house was sadly in favour of the devouring flames; the thick oak beams resisted manfully, letting themselves be charred externally, and retaining their sturdy heart untouched; but everything else was dry as tinder, and the flames, spurting upwards, with fury and velocity unequalled, licked greedily at the plaster and woodwork. Ceilings fell in with a crash, fine old furniture became a heap of tinder, iron rods and supports were bent as by the grasp of an infuriated Titan, and all the while, as though drunk with its own triumph, the fire grew and grew, and the lurid glare lit up the sky and startled the villages for miles around.

"Are we all here?" said Dick, looking about, his face pallid and drawn with anxiety.

"Every one, sir, thanks to your timely

warning," said the old butler, whose white locks waved in the hot blast.

" Thank God, then ; now let's try to save something." The drawing-room and gallery over it, Granny's old room, and the dining-room were helplessly burnt. It was there the fire had raged most fiercely, but the new wing in which Mrs. Vincent and the children had lived seemed as though it might be saved. The men redoubled their efforts. New recruits arrived every moment, and the fire-engine had at last made its appearance. There was a large incandescent flaming mass between the outside walls, which still stood grim and blackened, and the new wing, and, if it were possible to save the wing, the fire might possibly burn itself out in the molten cavern it had formed.

" It's the wind, the wind, I'm afraid of," said the old gardener, looking anxiously towards the west, " it seems to be rising."

Just then the flames gave a mocking leap, and darted across. In a moment the new wing was in flames.

" Oh, my jewels ! my jewels," shrieked Mrs. Vincent, " save them, somebody—save them."

" Where are they ? " asked Dick, standing close beside her.

" In my room. Oh ! the flames are terrible ; see in another moment my room will be burnt."

" I will get them if it is in man's power," said Dick rushing towards the burning mass. He had forgotten Mrs. Vincent's property in his great desire to save the pictures, which, cut hastily out of their frames, were cast on the ground, amid a motley heap of furniture and plate dashed from the windows, and saved to the best of each man's ability. But to Mrs. Vincent her little possessions, her trinkets and jewels, were as precious as the family heir-looms to Dick. In a fit of self-reproach he determined to rescue them, himself. It was no easy task ; the flames, scarcely intimidated by the showers of water poured on them, rioted sublimely in their fearlessness. Had it not been a dreadful it would have been a sublime sight. The great sheet of flame dancing and quivering with bacchanalian delight, the tongues of fire leaping up in wild ecstacy to fall back in sullen intensity of power, the group of helpless creatures battling with the awful strength of the consuming elements, and with white despairing faces ironically tinged with rosy hues, watching each fresh advance and victory of the fire. It was easy to get into the wing by the back door, but to make his way into Mrs. Vincent's room needed all Dick's courage and daring. He had to tread on burning floors, and he felt the scorching heat seize his hair and moustache. Outside, the breathless crowd viewed him in silence. They could distinguish the black figure cautiously feeling its way and fitfully illuminated at intervals by gleams and flashes of light: now lost to view for a moment behind a pillar or a rafter, then emerging, still steadily advancing; he was on the threshold of Mrs. Vincent's room, and now he was in it. A shout of applause arose. Dick groped his way about. In another instant he had the jewel-case in his hand, but as he turned to the door a sheet of flame and smoke swept in and hid him from the affrighted spectators. Some of the maids swooned. This was too terrible; to risk one's life for jewels, seemed to them almost profane.

"Throw me a rope," cried Dick, suddenly

appearing at the window, blackened with
smoke, yet apparently safe and sound. A
ladder was brought and put up against the
wall. "A rope, a rope!" shouted Dick
again. No one could remember where such
a thing was to be found. "A rope," again
shouted Dick, and he stood there, like a young
hero outlined against the cruel leaping flame.
Then a crash was heard and the women hiding
their faces cried "Oh!" with a long-drawn
shudder. It was only a bit of the wall
crumbling. Dick still stood at the window
waiting. He had torn in strips and knotted
together some sheets and let them down, but
they were too short, a leap thence to the
ground would still be dangerous. A cry
of anger rose from the group below, "Where
is a rope? Do bring a rope." As usual in
such cases no one remembered where anything was to be found; the butler knew
there were ropes on the premises, but could
not state where; the gardener thought they
were in the loft, and hither and thither each
one ran, frightened, bewildered, and helpless.
And all this time Dick stood at the window,
and the flames gained upon him, and the
heat was almost intolerable, and there

seemed no way of escape, but death on all
sides. If he waited, certain death ; if he
jumped, probable death. "Jump," was the
cry from below now, "you had better
jump." He saw a blanket stretched by
willing arms beneath him, he gazed into
anxious eager faces. He knew they would
save him if they could, and yet he hesitated.
Just then a burning blast touched his face,
his clothes were on fire, his hands smarting
with pain. He still held the dressing-case
in his hand. "Accursed thing!" he thought,
"shall I die for you ?" and Luce's face rose
before him in the angry flame, and her eyes
so clear and deep looked reproachfully, as
they had done that night at the opera.
"Catch it," he shouted as he tossed the
dressing-case on the ground. It burst open
from the shock, and cases of diamonds and
pearls fell at the feet of stable-men and
gardeners, who, never heeding, still held the
blanket, and still shouted to him "jump."
He was feeling giddy, the heat and smoke
were choking him, but he had saved the
jewels at least, he had not died a coward.
Perhaps, after all, this was as good an ending

to his life as he could have dared to hope for. They were coming nearer, nearer, in their devilish gracefulness and strength— the hungry flames; what pain, what fearful heat, he could endure it no longer! "Oh! God, have mercy on me!" he cried out. Then he jumped.

CHAPTER XIV.

In the cool clear morning light, the great
pile of buildings stood a blackened ruin.
The strongly-built walls resisted the fire, but
the heart of the structure had melted away,
and showed only a hideous chasm. Some of
the furniture, and most of the pictures and
plate, were saved, and Mrs. Vincent's jewel-
case; but Dick, the hero of the affair, the
man who had risked life and limb, lay
terribly injured and unconscious in the
bailiff's house, whither he had been carried
after his accident. Mrs. Vincent scarcely knew
whether to mourn or to rejoice. *If* anything happened to Dick the inheritance was
her husband's, and yet that he should have
risked his life and perhaps lost it for her
was a terrible idea. She tried to comfort
herself and still the vain upheavings of her

desire by repeating that one must conform to the decrees of Providence, that He knew best, that Dick's fate lay in His hands, and so forth, but inwardly she was possessed by a febrile anxiety, and watched every symptom of his condition with unceasing interest and never-failing acumen. The rest of the family picnicked as best they could amid bales of furniture and piles of chairs and tables and picture-frames, heaped together just as they had been rescued. There were no regular meals and everything took place in delightful confusion. Dolly and Eliza were enchanted. It was the nearest approach to romance they had ever experienced in their uneventful lives, and they made the most of the opportunity. They dressed themselves in all kinds of odds and ends and wandered about hand-in-hand amid the smoking ruins, expecting to find some valuable treasure in their midst. Glass smoked till it looked like bronze, opaline crystals formed from the action of the heat, molten lead run into the most grotesque shapes, rewarded their search, but the treasure lay only in their imagination. But the poor old butler had dis

covered something. Being considered too
weak to hold the blanket, he had stood by
anxiously at the time of the incident of the
dressing-case, and, as it burst open by the
violence of the fall, he hurried forward to
collect the fragments. He picked up the
various cases and some of their contents,
and as he did so noticed a packet wrapped
in white paper, with the seals broken, and
addressed to Lady Fenchurch. The super-
scription puzzled the old man for the
moment, then, as all the facts flashed on his
memory, he put the packet in his pocket,
and gathering up the rest of the valuables
hurried the dressing-case into a safe corner.
Mrs. Vincent, distracted between the intensity of her observation of Dick's movements
and her desire to obtain safe possession of
her jewels, had not noticed the old man's
manœuvres, and when the jewel-case was
finally shown to her as safe, though somewhat damaged by the fall, she made only a
hasty survey of its contents. Meanwhile
the old butler, having examined the packet
and satisfied himself that it contained the
pearl necklace, kept his own counsel and
determined to say nothing until Dick was

sufficiently recovered to understand the importance of the discovery.

The news of the disaster, coupled with a very exaggerated description of Dick's dangerous condition, reached the inmates of Oakdene through the servants' gossip. The butcher had told the cook, who had told the butler, who thought it his duty to communicate the intelligence to Miss Fenchurch. The old maid was dreadfully shocked. She hurried into her sister-in-law's boudoir, where she was busily decorating the pug with a new scarlet ribbon.

" Oh, Evelyn! your new home, and poor Mr. Carrol, oh, dear! and all the fine old furniture too ——"

" What has happened, Rachel ? " said Lady Fenchurch, rising quickly and upsetting the pug somewhat rudely on to the floor, " you really should spare my nerves a little, especially as I did not sleep well last night."

" My dear, I am so sorry." Miss Fenchurch sank breathlessly into a chair. "But then fires do not happen every day ; it is the first bad one I remember in all my experience."

"Fire! what fire?" Evelyn turned a shade whiter than was her wont.

"Well, really I don't know; they say Long Leam is burnt to the ground; nothing left but a heap of ashes; and Mr. Carrol, after doing wonders to save everything and everybody, is dying from the result of fearful wounds."

"Dying!—how horrible!"

"Yes, my dear, and burns are such terrible agony. I remember, when Sally Brown's child was scalded by the tea-kettle, her shrieks were awful to listen to."

"We must go at once, Rachel."

"Go where, my dear?"

"To see Mr. Carrol. Here, I'll order the carriage immediately. Smith can be round in a quarter-of-an-hour; and you go and put your bonnet on."

"And your nerves?"

"They are all right—I shan't break down."

"But, my dear, you are a young widow, and no one knows anything of your relation to Mr. Carrol. It would be indecent —positively indecent and unwomanly—I couldn't countenance it, my dear; I couldn't indeed—not with my dear dead brother's widow."

"Unwomanly! indecent!" Evelyn walked up and down passionately; "when, perhaps, for the only time in my life, I wish to do a right and an unselfish thing! Do you think *I* like sickness and suffering, and, perhaps, death?—I loathe it—I shrink from it. I could run away from it, and yet I must go. Remember, I am to marry this man."

"But not yet, my dear; not till a decent period of mourning has elapsed—what will people say?"

"Decent period of mourning! Am I to wait till my crape is worn out, to help a fellow-creature? besides"—suddenly changing her tone, "just think; I have never seen a fire; and it must be *so* interesting."

"A morbid love of excitement," moaned Miss Fenchurch; "a purely morbid love of excitement! What are the young women of the present day coming to? Ah! if you would only knit, my dear, it is so steadying to the nerves."

"No doubt; no doubt"—Lady Fenchurch stamped her foot impatiently; "but I'm going now—do you mean to come?"

Poor Miss Fenchurch sighed. She wished she had never reported the butcher's conversation, for, after all, it might not be true; but, like a docile dog, she followed Evelyn upstairs, and prepared to put on her things. During the drive Lady Fenchurch was in an unwonted state of excitement. She could not help feeling the unconventionality of her proceeding, and, at the same time, enjoying it with the geniality of a school-girl. She was so tired of the trappings of woe, and of the necessity for quiet retirement, that this totally unexpected excitement tickled her nerves pleasantly.

The day was bright and fresh; the golden corn waved in the fields, ready for the reaper's sickle; the blue sky, dappled with clouds, arched high and light above their heads; the scented hedges, the profusion of wild flowers, offered an agreeable prospect to their eyes, and made the contrast between the present and the future even more dreadful. An old home in ruins, a dying man, her own sad fortune, were not agreeable subjects of meditation, and yet, as she drove along, Evelyn's spirits rose, spite of herself. Miss Fenchurch gloomed in silence. She had never before been called upon to play propriety on such an occasion as this.

" Do you think he will know me ? " asked Evelyn, suddenly.

" Know you ? I suppose he will have his head tied up in a bandage with ice upon it. You are surely not going to penetrate into the young man's bedroom ? "

" I shall go to Dick, wherever he may be."

" Humph ! " ejaculated Miss Fenchurch ; " no young woman in my day ever presumed so much as to know that a young man *had* a bedroom. That kind of subject was always slurred over with propriety."

" You forget I am a widow, and not an old maid," wickedly said Evelyn.

" Yes, my dear, I know that ; and I know also what St. Paul says in the matter."

" Please don't quote St. Paul ; besides, here we are ——"

The lodge-gates stood open ; crowds of people paraded the park, and there in the distance, where the handsome old house used to be, the black walls reared themselves gaunt and lonely. Beyond, the grove was intact, and the light-footed Mercury still poised himself in the attitude of flight on the golden base amidst the dark-green foliage.

"Oh, Rachel, it is dreadful! and to think we lunched here only yesterday, and I chose my own room — the one with the western aspect," said Evelyn, standing up in the carriage to see better.

"I wonder if it was heavily insured; of course all that old furniture and the Adams carving is gone for ever," said the old maid, "besides half the time the insurance offices dispute your claim."

They drove up at that instant, and a civil policeman answered their inquiries.

"Mr. Carrol is very bad, I believe," he said, "but you'll find them all down at the bailiff's house there—it's only a few hundred yards off." He pointed with his finger, and the carriage drove on. Both the ladies were silent, wrapped in their own thoughts. The bailiff's house was a pretty one. It was built of red brick with white stone copings; it had a nice orchard on one side, and a poultry-yard on the other, and over the door climbed a splendid pear-tree. No one was to be seen, for Dolly and Eliza were as usual groping about the ruins. Uncle Vincent was away superintending the removal of furniture, and Mrs. Vincent was making up accounts in the back parlour, which looked out on the farmyard. The footman rang the bell, and after a little a scared maid appeared, whose wits, scattered by the sad events of the previous night, had not yet returned to their habitual calm of stupidity.

"Madam—Mrs. Vincent — Mr. Carrol— oh, yes, they're all at home," she stammered. "Please will you walk in here?"

Miss Fenchurch directed the coachman to put up at the nearest inn, and then the two ladies entered the house. Lady Fenchurch's heart beat violently. She dreaded any horrible sight, and was not quite sure whether she cared enough for Dick to endure his mangled, perhaps bleeding, appearance. He had been so handsome; how if the beauty had disappeared, and given place to loathsome ugliness. How should she dare to look?

The little maid showed them into the front parlour, fitted with glossy old oak cupboards and tables. Miss Fenchurch went into ecstasy over their polished surfaces and

handsome carving, while Evelyn thought-
fully smelt at a bunch of roses and mignonette stuck in a brown jug in the centre
of the table. Presently the maid returned,
ushering in a nurse.

" You want to see Mr. Carrol, ladies ?" she
said. " I fear it is impossible. He is unconscious."

" Just for one minute," said Lady Fenchurch, pleadingly ; " just for one minute let
us see him."

The nurse hesitated. This handsome
young lady was no doubt some relation or
cousin or a sweetheart. The presence of a
pretty woman could not hurt him, especially
as he took no notice of what was going on
around him, and it would please her.

" Very well, then," she said ; " I will risk
it, but you must promise not to speak or
make any noise."

" I promise," and therewith leaving Miss
Fenchurch to a further contemplation of the
old oak they mounted the stairs. The sick
room was shaded, and only a gentle light
filtered through the green Venetian blinds.
In the bed lay Dick pale as death, and
motionless. A smell of ether and lavender-

water floated in the air, but there was nothing terrible or frightening. Dick's face was perfectly calm. He might have been asleep. Evelyn breathed more freely. She little knew how much she had dreaded till her fears were relieved. She drew near, and gently put her lips to the cheek which lay wearily on the white pillow. As she did so the invalid moved and murmured softly, " Luce."

She started back as if stung by a viper, while the nurse remarked with satisfaction— " That is the first time he has spoken yet— he is getting better."

Lady Fenchurch gave another look, a half-frightened, half angry look, towards the bed.

" Let us go down, nurse; there is a smell of ether in the room. I can't bear it."

The nurse opened the door quietly, thinking to herself that it was a pity young ladies should be so sensitive; she never minded the smell, or indeed far worse odours.

" There, now, my dear, you're as white as a ghost," said Miss Fenchurch, when she returned to the little parlour. " I knew it would upset you to see the poor young man, and in bed too. People always look worse in bed."

"You were right and I was wrong," said Evelyn, in a faint voice, sinking into a chair. "Let us go home."

"What? without seeing the Vincents and the ruins. I thought we came partly to see the ruins; I am much interested to observe the ravages of the fire—I am sure it was caused by the housemaids' candles, they are so careless."

"Very well." Evelyn resigned herself feebly to the consequence of her own imprudence.

"You do not require my services any further," said the nurse, who was still standing in the aperture of the door, with her hand on the lock. "I should like to return to my patient. Just now he showed some signs of consciousness."

"No, my good woman, you can go—at least—you must first tell us what you think of him, is he likely to recover?"

Evelyn sat by stonily. She did not even lift her eyes at the question.

"It's impossible to say; if he takes nourishment, and if he keeps quiet, he may do. But we are afraid of internal injuries."

" Internal injuries ! " echoed Evelyn, despairingly; " how terrible ! "

" Yes, ma'am, and it's a wonder he escaped with his life at all.   He was dreadfully burnt, and all shattered to pieces like."

" Have you often had a case like this before ? " asked Miss Fenchurch, moved by female curiosity to discuss the case as one of pathological interest.

" Not exactly, but I've had a good deal to do with burns and accidents."

" We are keeping nurse, and she ought to return to her patient," observed Evelyn.

" Yes, of course; but, nurse, you're not afraid of delirium, are you ? "

" No, ma'am.   He seems quiet enough, quite child-like I may say."

" Well, take great care of him, his life is very valuable.   He is the master of Long Leam, you know."

" So I understand," and the nurse, pursing her lips, withdrew quietly.

" And what do you mean to do now, Rachel ? " said Lady Fenchurch, rousing herself from the apathy into which she seemed to have fallen.

"Mrs. Vincent will be here directly and we must offer her assistance; this little house must be most inconvenient for so large a party. What do you say to asking them all over to Oakdene?"

"What! those tiresome girls, Dolly and Eliza?—I could not stand them."

"They are very much like other girls, I think, and seem quiet and ladylike ——"

"They are fearfully dull—fancy having those girls on one's hands all day."

"Well, they will learn to employ themselves, I cannot see any great hardship in that ——"

"And that dreadful Mr. Vincent."

"He will be *your* uncle soon if the poor young man recovers; hush! ——" Miss Fenchurch drew herself up primly; "here comes Mrs. Vincent."

CHAPTER XV.

Mrs. Vincent entered with her cap-strings flying and an air of unwonted gloom and solemnity. "How kind of you to come," she said, "into this house of mourning!"

"I suppose the insurance is all right," put in Miss Fenchurch, quickly.

"I *hope* so, but one never knows. That beautiful house, Miss Fenchurch—that fine old mansion that we were all so fond of—burnt to the ground—the ways of Providence are past finding out."

"And the housemaids?" ejaculated Miss Fenchurch, "oh! those housemaids — are you convinced the fire did not originate in dropped lucifer matches?"

"Very probably, but —— "

"Or with lighted papers thrown into

the fire-place? that is another dangerous habit. I write up warnings in all the bed-rooms."

"Rachel, what does it matter *how* the fire originated? the question is what to do now."

"Yes; can we offer you beds—we have no one at home, you know, but ourselves."

"Thanks, there is poor young Dick, my duty is to the unfortunate lad —— "

"But your husband and daughters."

"Ah, Dolly and Eliza—they must go home—they must learn to submit to the decrees of Providence. I shall arrange for them to start to-morrow."

"What a head for organization you must have!" said Miss Fenchurch, admiringly.

Mrs. Vincent smiled a sad little self-con-scious smile, "I have been told so."

"And you are an admirable nurse, I am sure."

"I have nursed all my family. And who is there that has not been ill and can look forward to perpetual good health?"

"Very true." Miss Fenchurch sighed also.

Evelyn, whom this colloquy exasperated, said, "We had better not detain Mrs. Vin-cent now, Rachel, if we can do no more for her, and she has all her arrangements to make."

"But you will see the ruins first—oh yes, you must, please; my girls are always there; children, you know, perfect children, and yet so accomplished; if you will come with me you need not be incommoded by any crowd—they all know *me*."

Therewith Mrs. Vincent rang for the half-scared maid, who in all her time of service with the quiet bailiff's wife (who of her own accord was now relegated to the kitchen premises) had never seen such goings on and such a quantity of fine folk, and laid upon her such numerous and urgent injunctions about hot water, luncheon, the making of beef-tea and lemonade, that the poor girl's wits almost forsook her again. Then, gathering up her mantle and a garden-hat, she sallied forth to pilot her guests. Mrs. Vincent was a very important person now, and the respectful bows and greetings of the work-people they met amply denoted it. As long as the young master lay ill and dying, and Mr. Vincent scarcely realised his position, every duty and responsibility devolved upon his wife, and admirably she responded to them. She was happier than she had been for many a long day, walking about the smoking ruins and giving orders to the nurse in the shaded sick room. Presently they met Dolly and Eliza, their hands full of calcined stones and queer-shaped bits of glass and lead. "We have found such strange things," they exclaimed simultaneously, "and over there they are digging out all manner of funny twisted bits of iron, and books and glass as black as coal —do come mamma."

The girls were quite excited. They felt like Robinson Crusoe on his desert island. Flurried with happy expectation and surprise, they had quite forgotten their company manners, left their gloves behind, and looked for the nonce two joyous sunburnt simple English girls.

"Dolly! Eliza!" said their mother, "take these ladies and show them everything; where is your father—find him."

"Papa is in the stables, he is talking to the grooms about the narrow escape the horses had."

"There, that will do, don't chatter, and behave properly," added Mrs. Vincent; "and when you have *quite* satisfied your curiosity, Lady Fenchurch, I hope you will come back to lunch."

"Thank you, no," said Evelyn, a little proudly—war was secretly accepted between these two women—they already mutually disliked and feared each other; "we must be going home."

"But we will come to take the last news of your dear and interesting patient before we drive off," said Miss Fenchurch, with her old-fashioned maidenly punctiliousness.

"Dear and interesting patient," mumbled Mrs. Vincent to herself, as she hurried back to the bailiff's little house; "will he live or will he die? that is the question. I wish I knew. I wish I could gather some definite notion of the safest line of conduct. Those women scent something, they mean mischief, they are after him, I believe, and the young one looks as if she wouldn't be trifled with; as for the other, of course she's an old goose."

Mrs. Vincent knew nothing of Evelyn's short visit to the sick room, and the nurse never told her, thinking very properly that she had rather transgressed directions in

admitting a stranger. Had Mrs. Vincent
known this, she would have descried even
more danger in the subtly-veiled politeness
of the ladies' invitation to Oakdene. She
was considerably disturbed too by the absence of the pearl necklace, which in setting
to rights her dressing-case she discovered to
be missing, but she dared not proclaim her
loss, and only trusted that the obnoxious
jewel had perished in the flames, and thus
extricated her from any further dilemma.

Mrs. Vincent walked softly into the sick
room. The nurse had gone to her dinner.
There was no one present but the invalid,
and he lay with his eyes shut as if he were
dead. Was he dead? Perhaps. Mrs. Vincent stooped and laid her hand on his forehead, as softly as Evelyn had laid her lips,
but there was no love in her touch. The
sick man seemed to feel it, he moved and
moaned while her hard, cold eyes looked
critically at him. Why couldn't he die
when he was maimed and mangled, already
a semi-corpse? He would not feel death
now; its bitterest pangs were past, and his
removal might do such good to her children.
The doctor scarcely expected him to live

everything would be smooth and natural if he were gone. She need have no secret to keep then, be tortured by no fears lest he should discover her deceit and revenge it.

Why shouldn't that pale figure grow paler and whiter, and the heart stop, and the spirit fly away—where? Oh, that was not her business; but she loved her children, and in a kind of contemptuous way the drunken husband too, and Dick's death would be their gain. The leaves of the wide-spreading pear-tree flapped gently against the window, the summer breeze swept through the crevices of the blind, and Dick lay motionless. His life hung there by a thread, trembling in the balance of eternity. A small sedative, a few drops of an opiate, and he would never awaken more. No one could call it a crime, rather it seemed a mercy to spare the poor wretch the agony of convalescence or the worse pains of prolonged death. What will not a woman do when she is tempted by herself? That self, that venal monitor, persuades more surely than lies in the power of any external influence. The head speaks more surely and to more purpose than the heart. While Mrs.

Vincent wrought her vague wishes into firm intentions the door opened softly, and the nurse entered, rosy from her dinner. She looked doubtfully at Mrs. Vincent; is not the soul visible in the countenance? Then glanced towards the bed. "Our dear patient is better, I think," said Mrs. Vincent, in her cold, dry voice, "but he seems inclined to be quiet. You had better let him sleep."

CHAPTER XVI.

LUCE stood with clasped hands in the shadow of the window-curtain. She wanted to be alone, for she felt her heart breaking. That morning she had heard the news. Long Leam was a heap of cinders, and Dick lay dying. Dying! impossible. She could only see him as he looked when they parted, so happy, so young, so beautiful, with such a spell of pleasant years to run out before him. Those bright blue eyes, that graceful figure, so tall and strong, with the confidence of youth straightening its lithe gait, crushed, mangled, shapeless. Ah, it could not be. She twisted her handkerchief between her hands and bit her lips till the blood came. All the love she had tried to stifle in her heart broke forth like a long dammed torrent. In sickness, in death, he seemed nearer to her. She was almost mad with longing, she hungered so for one little glimpse of the poor broken body, to whom perhaps she could bring relief. If he must die why could she not be with him, minister to his wants, turn his pillow, give him to drink? No one knew what he liked so well as she did. But she was nothing to him now, nothing, not half so much as his faithful old terrier, or the servant that nursed and sat up with him. And it was all her own doing, all her own, no one to blame but herself. An agonized yearning stole over her. Perhaps he could be saved; if any one *could* save him, she would. Again she clenched her hands. She remembered Lady Eleanor and the proprieties. She was hemmed in on all sides by her own actions and by the sphere in which she was placed. Something whispered to her she had done right, and then in another instant she said to herself passionately that there was no such thing as right, that love was everything, that love was too sacred, too precious, to be lightly cast away. He had not loved *her* much perhaps but she had loved him, he had laid his kisses on her lips, he had pressed her in his arms. And, though tortured by jealousy, burning with hopeless, unrequited affection, she had yielded up these things to another. And where was that other, was she by his side, sitting patiently as behoved woman, cooling his fevered head, wiping away the death-sweat, holding his hand, passing with him through the last dread hours, or was she nursing her own fears, and leaving him to hired cares? Luce knew what would be Mrs. Vincent's tender mercies, she could gauge the depths of *her* pity. If he were consigned to *that!* Luce started up. Perhaps he was alone and wanted her. She would go, so gladly, she asked nothing but just to be near him. The rolling carriages outside, hurrying to their business and their pleasure, insatiable in their voracity for frivolous amusement, recalled her to a sense of reality. Dick would die, and she would never see him again. People would ring out his praises, talk of him for an hour, pity him, and then he would be forgotten. It was terrible to die so young, and to be forgotten. She leant against the window-curtain, looking out with hollow glassy eyes at the street below.

More people, gaily moving,—they did not care, no one cared except the little girl up there in the bed-room, her white face staring into space, who was parted from him.

"Luce!" called Maud's gay voice beside her, Maud whom no misadventures daunted. "Luce, are you not coming down? I have so much to tell you."

"I don't want to hear it." Luce put her fingers in her ear.

"Nonsense! don't be stupid. I'm going to be married at last."

"Married!" The word seemed to Luce to have no meaning; wedding-cake, and favours, and pretty presents, were incongruous and distasteful, while Dick lay dying.

"Yes, of course, why shouldn't I? Arthur Sterney has proposed at last, and he has promised to give up the burlesque actresses, and live nicely and economically, and his old aunt is going to pay his debts. She always said he had the best of hearts, only his head was not quite so good."

"What is the use of a heart?"

"Use of a heart? well, it makes a man

kind and generous. Arthur means to give
me lovely presents ; a good-hearted man
always gives presents."

" And, if he breaks your heart, what will
you do ? "

" Bless you, child, my heart is not easily
broken ; it has certainly been cracked a few
times, but I've had it strongly riveted.   I
have no fear. I am quite equal to most
men and have studied their natures pro-
foundly.   They are not, like us, swayed by
no end of motives, impenetrable and mixed
motives ; you can generally trace a man's
actions to their root—himself. Now if you've
only got the root you can easily plant and
water and make it grow. Man-gardening is as
easy as window-gardening; give them plenty
of scope, deep earth, you know, and don't be
impatient or always pulling them up by the
roots to see why the flower doesn't come, and
you will easily reap the fruits."

" The flower is love, I suppose ? "

" No—I don't think so; love is rather
more of a weed. It grows rankly, and in
solitary places ; now you ——why, Luce !
you've been crying, and you've got a dug-

up look about you. Surely you're not fretting about that man still?"

"Hush! he is dying," said Luce, with warning up-lifted finger.

"Dying! poor fellow! I suppose you're very miserable?"

"Very." Luce hid her face in Maud's dress. Even so lukewarm a friendship comforted her at that instant.

"And I daresay now you are filled with some Quixotic kind of notion that you would like to go and nurse him?"

Luce hung her head.

"And, of course, save his life, and make him eternally grateful. I know the sort of thing. My dear, that kind of melodramatic nonsense only does for the stage."

"Think, just think—if he is dying?"

"Luce, you surprise me. With all your quiet and mouse-like ways, you have a great deal of poetry in you; and yet, when you had the chance of marrying this man, you deliberately threw it away."

"Oh! cannot you understand?" sobbed Luce. "I loved him so, that I wanted him to be noble. I thought my love would raise him to the height I fancied he could reach.

Ah! I see it now; it was all visionary, and stupid, and high-strung; and he is just dying, and I am here, helpless and alone."

"Well! I confess I cannot conceive your kind of love; but I do see you are unhappy, dear; what can I do for you?"

Maud spoke kindly, and her commonplace words soothed Luce undefinably. When nature asserts her claim, when souls are really stirred, there runs a kind of sympathetic chain from one to the other; but yet we never absolutely touch each other at all points. There remain depths hidden from the subtlest divining, and chords that can never be struck; so that when we suffer most, we are always really and spiritually alone. Yet the magic of a kindly touch, the affinity of a presence, the tremble of a voice, speak to us of happiness, and raise our drooping spirits to a possibility of better things. It is in this that the communion of friends is truly beneficial; we idealise their comprehension; we misconstrue their grasp of the truth, and even our mistakes serve to heal our sorrowing hearts.

"What can I do?" repeated Maud.

"Oh! if you could persuade my aunt to

return to Highview! there we should be nearer him, more able to know, and perhaps to help."

" Well, Luce, to show you I am not ill-natured, now that I am engaged to be married, and don't so much care for London (I shall have plenty of time to choose my dresses), I will urge our return. Your aunt is unusually good-tempered to-day. I suppose you would like to go home at once ? "

Luce nodded her head.

" I will try what I can do," said Maud encouragingly, as she left the room.

She did try her best, and soon came back with Lady Eleanor's affirmative answer. The season was nearly over, Lady Eleanor opined, Maud's engagement had reached a satisfactory termination, and as to Luce, there seemed very little reason to suppose that town or country would make any difference to her prospects, so they might go as soon as they pleased she added. Luce and Maud started first, and arrived at Highview only a few days after the fire at Long Leam. Maud lent herself amiably to Luce's desires, and the two girls concocted quite a little plot together. They were to drive into

West Thorpe at the earliest opportunity in Luce's small pony cart, and, under pretext of shopping, to remain there a couple of hours while they sent a messenger to Long Leam to make inquiries about Mr. Carrol's health. Maud enjoyed anything in the shape of intrigue heartily, and Luce was too utterly downcast and wretched to care for aught but the driblet of news she might by this means obtain. They were thus agreed; and Luce, with the prospect of certain intelligence before her, ventured to feel a little happier.

The next few days were uneventful enough. They dared not drive to West Thorpe every day for fear of attracting attention, and each report of the invalid seemed more discouraging.

" It is a slow kind of thing, you know, when you're all smashed up as that poor creature is," Maud tried to assure her friend, " one mustn't expect progress. Every day he *lives* is a day gained."

" Ought one even to wish for life if he suffers so ? " said Luce despondingly.

" Well that depends. I suppose everyone

values life, even the cripples, and the deaf and dumb."

"It would be terrible for him to be a cripple," said Luce as they drove down the leafy lanes; "I can never imagine him except in the fullest health and spirits."

"Ah! that's it, and people always pity you far more if you have enjoyed good health all your life, while the poor invalid gets no sympathy because he has already suffered so much. It's a queer world, that's what it is, and most things are topsy-turvy in it."

"I can imagine this world so beautiful, that it might seem like paradise."

"You mean if one has just the things one wishes for, but nobody has. Look at me, now, I'm quite content, and think myself lucky to get Arthur Sterney for a husband; and yet, what with his debts, and his duns, and the way in which he is bored, unless he finds constant amusement, you wouldn't think him such a very desirable husband after all."

"Why do you marry him then?" asked Luce, idly flicking a fly off the pony's back with her whip.

"You really need not ask such ridiculous questions. You know perfectly well that there are more women than men in the world; that to those of us poor creatures who can't emigrate as housemaids, or set up as lady doctors, there is very little scope given; and, my dear, I think that girl is not so great a fool who makes the best of life, even if it is not very good, as her friend who stands out for sympathy and love and all the paraphernalia of sentiment."

Luce quivered. Her companion's philosophy cut deep into her heart, and there were times when she said to herself that the children of this world were at least wise in their generation. They knew positively what they wanted, and they strove for it, if not nobly, at least perseveringly—the secret of success.

Presently Maud spoke again.

"You get paler and thinner every day, Luce; if you don't take care you will be ill too. Can't you rouse yourself? Find some occupation. I know you don't care for dress or gossip as I do, but your music need not be quite neglected."

"Never mind me," said Luce, with a new touch of fretful impatience. "Do you think she is with him?"

They had gleaned but little information from the messenger, who only saw the bulletin at the door, which said Mr. Carrol was no better, and gave no other details. Luce would fain have known how Dick slept, who was with him, and every little item of sick-room tittle-tattle.

" I should think not ! " answered Maud, composedly. " Remember she is a widow, and will probably take very good care of her reputation, now, as she risked it once. Unless she announces her engagement to him, which would shock all the good people, how can she nurse a young man—what reason can she give ? "

The good sense of Maud's remarks left Luce no pretext for demur, and she accustomed herself to think of Dick as alone. Presently, by one of the illogical leaps that love occasionally makes, she imagined herself with him, and was able to piece together fragments of the conversation they might hold.

Mr. Highview, coming in from his ride one evening, gave form and stability to her cogitations. It was generally assumed in the family that Luce, having given her lover his *congé*, could not care for him, and that his affairs might therefore be discussed with impunity in her presence.

People will judge our private feelings and prejudices in this manner, according to their conception of probability.

"Very sad about young Carrol, I must say!" he remarked, pouring himself out a cup of tea.

"What has happened?" said Lady Eleanor, languidly. "I suppose he will not lose much; the house must have been well insured."

"He may lose his life though—I don't expect *that* was insured."

"His life!" Luce sat with parted lips, breathless.

"He is as bad as possible. I hear Pilule telegraphed to-day to London for a physician; they can't keep the fever down."

"I believe Mrs. Vincent is an excellent nurse," said Lady Eleanor. "I know she attended ambulance classes, and boasted to everybody how well she could put on a bandage."

"Well, I suspect this is a little beyond her capacity."

"Is Mrs. Vincent his only nurse?" asked Maud, responding to a pleading look from Luce.

"I believe so; she will look after him, I expect. A fine managing woman, though she didn't behave quite well about the affair of the necklace. But women are always so prejudiced; and, besides, she could not go against her husband."

"Why, his death would be her gain," said Maud, hotly. "I don't see how you can expect her *really* to care, and to take much trouble."

"Oh! my dear," reproved Mr. Highview, "she is too high-minded not to do her duty."

"Mrs. Vincent is very fond of her own interests," persisted Maud.

"Now, my dear, what you say there is really shocking; why should we suspect Mrs. Vincent of these unnatural thoughts?"

"She has thin lips, and flat bandeaux of greasy hair; I always mistrust people with those peculiarities."

Lady Eleanor laughed. "Maud, you put things so funnily," she said.

"Well, I pity poor Dick Carrol while he

is in her clutches. I declare, as I am his cousin, I think I will go over and offer my services as nurse. I am sure he would prefer my soft blundering hands to her bony claws."

In the general derision Maud's announcement caused, Luce escaped to her room. Hot tears sprang to her eyes, and the pain she was enduring seemed more and more intolerable.

CHAPTER XVII.

Lady Fenchurch did not repeat her visit to Long Leam. Whenever Miss Fenchurch broached the subject Evelyn seemed to shrink within herself.

"But really, it is rather heartless of us not to go and inquire, and the weather is so fine, too," said the old maid regretfully.

"We can telegraph or write. That will do."

"For your intended husband?"

"As I must not announce to the world that he *is* my intended husband, I cannot see that it matters; besides he is semi-delirious, he cannot know."

"Well, I think we might call to inquire without risk of being considered intrusive," murmured Miss Fenchurch, "and I really cannot understand you; you were so keen at one time to visit Mr. Carrol, when, myself, I thought it a little indecorous."

Evelyn kept silence.

" Is not that true, my dear ? "

" Perhaps, but I wish you would not worry me." She shivered. " I think I have got a chill."

" I am afraid you sat out too late in the garden last evening, and you would not put on your shawl."

" The moon was lovely, and it is really only pleasant in the evening. What did you tell me Mr. Peter Fenchurch wrote to you about ? "

" I will read you his letter at once," and herewith the old maid promptly displayed a piece of paper.

" You see he writes from London ; he says he has been travelling in America, and only just received the news of my poor brother's death. He writes very properly, very properly indeed, considering that I do not believe he ever saw my poor brother. Ah, well, if this dear place must go to a stranger I am at least glad that he should be a person of nice feeling."

"He ought to be very glad; he will be rich and master of this place."

"Yes, my dear; and I think we ought to receive him kindly."

"Is he coming here?"

"Well, he says he should like to pay his respects to me; we can scarcely refuse that."

"And will he bring his wife and his large family?"

"No. It seems from his letter that his wife is dead, and he does not speak of any children."

"He is elderly, I suppose?"

"Oh, yes, he must be elderly, for I remember Hilary telling me he came to Eton just as Hilary left Cambridge. There could not be more than ten years between them."

"I daresay he is a tiresome and uninteresting person."

"I don't quite see why you should say that, dear; he must have some of the family characteristics about him."

"And then of course he will be excellent," put in Evelyn, mockingly.

"Well, my dear, at any rate we must prepare for his reception."

"Oh, I daresay he will be satisfied with a cutlet and a glass of sherry if he has been travelling in wilds where he never got a letter. He can't be very particular."

"Which day shall I ask him?" said Miss Fenchurch, swelling with housewifely responsibility.

"Whenever you like. I am always here, you know. I am in mourning, so I can't go out."

Miss Fenchurch meekly accepted the ungracious permission, and, ruffled by the small excitement of receiving a strange guest, and yet one who would be near to her in various close and unpleasant ways, retired to the library to write her letter in the quiet of deep and mature consideration. It would not do to seem too eager, and yet she wished to be cordial; her dignity must not be forgotten, and yet a little curiosity might fairly be allowed to peep out. So Miss Fenchurch sat in solemn propriety, concocting her letter and learnedly trying the nibs of quill-pens upon her thumb-nail in order to find one of the requisite degree of softness. Lady Fenchurch, meanwhile, paced the garden in all the heat of noontide, shielded

only by her white parasol and utterly
regardless of the sun's power.

"That girl, that little plain girl," she
murmured, between her teeth, "to think
that her name should be on his lips when
he was lying there ill and helpless!" Lady
Fenchurch's *amour-propre* was deeply
wounded. Could it be that he had only
offered her his hand out of pity? The loving
days by the river when they glided in the
little boat over the rippling waters in a
peaceful haze of happiness, and thought of
nothing but their own enjoyment, seemed
so far away; the tragedy of her life had
obscured those memories, and made her
more cold and more practical. Yet if he
really only pitied and had ceased to love
her. It was intensely humiliating. No,
she would not go back and simulate tenderness, and bear disappointment any more,
until she knew the truth. How could little
plain Luce, for whom she had always felt a
kind of contemptuous pity, gain any real
hold on his affections. It was simply because
he was fickle and changeable and selfish, like
all men. She began to look about for a
way to extricate herself from the engage-

ment (she instinctively knew that he would
be too manly ever to seek to release himself),
and she found none. She could not give up
an iota of her wealth and her comforts, or
resign herself to the narrow life which would
satisfy her sister-in-law, and unless she
married Dick she saw no other outlet. True,
with her youth and beauty she might cap-
tivate some eligible person in the years to
come, but she was too prudent to risk the
substance for the shadow. It was better to
wait. Only one thing was impossible, to go
again and sit by that bedside and hear the
sick man's mumblings. Even the proposed
visit of Mr. Peter Fenchurch, dull and tiresome as he might be, would prove a certain
variety, and give her a valid excuse for
remaining at home. She amused herself by
speculating a little on Mr. Peter Fenchurch's
feelings when arriving one morning at the
post-office he found the letter conveying to
him the news that his elderly relation was
dead, and dying had bequeathed to him the
greater part of his fortune. Such an experience must be exceedingly delightful. No
such sweet surprise could ever come to her;
she was an orphan, a penniless woman, and

the widow of a man who by his testamen-
tary arrangements had even sought to
blacken her character. She walked a little
faster, and felt a sharp satisfaction in crunch-
ing the gravel beneath her feet. It seemed
as if she were stamping out her vindictive-
ness and burying it in the silent dust.

Miss Fenchurch, on the contrary, having
at last indited her letter, proceeded to examine the linen-cupboards in company with
the housemaid. She wished, as she expressed
it, that Mr. Peter Fenchurch should find
everything in perfect order, and be surprised at the quality of her housekeeping.
By her brother's will she was entitled to
everything she required in the shape of linen
and plate, but the remainder must be left in
such a condition that the carping eye could
find no fault. The best china too she dusted
lovingly with her own hands. There were
quantities of it, all put away in cupboards,
for it had never been the fashion to expose
china deliberately to the chances of clumsy
handling or to the dangers of modern *étagères*
and brackets. The china was carefully
washed once a year, and in the interim
reposed luxuriously on the deep shelves of

the vast closets where it was seen by no mortal, and could therefore be destroyed by no sacrilegious touch.

" Everything is right now, I think," said Miss Fenchurch, with a sigh. " There is not a fresh chip or a single crack in any of the cups, and I don't notice a leaf or a flower off the old Chelsea figures. Ah, Jane, if Mr. Peter Fenchurch should not care for china. What a calamity that would be!"

"It would indeed, ma'am, but I think most gentlefolks is partial to queer-shaped things; them dragons now, I suppose their beauty is their ugliness."

" Certainly," responded Miss Fenchurch, " they are very valuable Nankin china, and you must know that in the time of Queen Anne people of the highest quality approved only of monsters."

" Dear me, ma'am," said Jane, whose knowledge of history was a little vague, and who was not very sure whether Queen Anne lived before or after the Deluge. She was rather inclined to believe it was after, having heard something about antediluvian monsters in a hurried visit paid to the

Crystal Palace on bank holiday, "dear me, but then that was a very long time ago."

"Yes, indeed. Now, Jane, shut the cupboards, and give me the keys of the presses. I think I will go round and pay a visit to the dairy. Perhaps Mr. Peter may be a judge of butter and cheese. I am told in America they make tons of cheese and send it over to England to be sold as Cheshire and Gruyère."

CHAPTER XVIII.

THE old butler prized his discovery highly. He locked up the necklace in the plate-chest, where it was secure from thieves, and he took it out occasionally to look at it and see that it had not made wings for itself and flown away. He chuckled audibly as he thought how pleased the young master would be to see it, and what a thunder-bolt would fall upon Mrs. Vincent when it was generally known that the necklace which had caused his poor dear young master so much un-happiness had been all the while safely locked away in his aunt's dressing-case. "The wiper!" muttered the old man, as he cleaned his plate, " what she must ha' been made of to torment a poor young man like that, to lie and to cheat. Well, I'll be even with her ; " and the old man, who had

never forgiven Mrs. Vincent for her petty
economies and for her accusation regarding
the sherry, rejoiced greatly as he thought
of the humiliation in store for her. But as
the days went by, and every time he asked
to see his young master he was told that it
was impossible, for in his precarious condition *no one* must be admitted to the room,
he ceased to sing over his work, dropped
his chuckling, and finally had a morose fit;
strange dark thoughts oppressed him. He
owned little regard for Mrs. Vincent, he
believed her capable of almost anything,
and he began to suspect foul play. This
sick chamber, so hermetically closed that
not even an old servant might penetrate its
mysteries; the hired nurse, who, however
skilled, could not be supposed to entertain
much affection; the weird stories of violence
and delirium that filtered through shut doors,
increased and intensified his suspicions. Cups
of beef-tea and bottles of brandy certainly
returned empty from the patient's room, but
who could tell that any of the nourishment
had reached him? The butler had read his
Dickens to some purpose, and remembered
Mrs. Gamp. He grew feverishly anxious

("the young master," with his wild, careless
generous ways, had obtained a strange hold
over the hearts of his dependents); he listened
at doors, he got up in the middle of the
night to catch a sound or a muffled cry, and
hour by hour he became more and more
convinced that something uncanny was going
on. He tried to get the half-scared maid-
servant into his confidence, but she was too
scared to understand, and only answered
" Yes, sir," to all his queries. In despair
he sat down to think who could help him in
this dilemma; at last he remembered Bruce,
whose name had been kept prominently forward in the election, and determined to
summon him to his assistance. This required
to be performed in a somewhat roundabout
fashion, for no one in the house was acquainted
with his address; and several days elapsed
before he could obtain it from Mr. Highview, the only person he could think of as
possessing the desired information. When
at last he despatched the telegram, which,
began by presenting his humble duty, continued with the urgent request for Mr.
Bruce's presence, and ended by a mysterious intimation that something suspicious

was going on, the old man had expended
the sum of two shillings, and had fairly
mystified and alarmed the student. When
Bruce read in the paper the paragraph spe-
cially pointed out to him by his landlady,
who took the deepest interest in all the
places and people with whom he was connected, he had at once telegraphed to Dick
condoling with him and asking if he could
be of any assistance. Receiving no answer,
and being at that moment particularly engaged in hunting up an old authority on
some small point of old usage, he concluded
that Dick was well, busy, and did not require his services. When Mrs. Flinks again
brought him the paper, and bade him notice
the rumour of Dick's severe illness, he began
to grow alarmed, and the butler's telegram
received at that instant confirmed his worst
fears. He lost no time in answering, and
hastily stuffing a few things into a bag took
the next train to West Thorpe. It was
evening when he arrived. The lights were
burning in the sleepy little town, and a solitary
fly waited for the arrival of the train. The
horse was old and weak-kneed, the driver a
fossil, and the vehicle shaky and moulder-

ing; yet Bruce was heartily glad to find
even so unsatisfactory a conveyance. The
seven miles seemed an eternity, the night
was dark and damp, light rain was falling,
the hedges looked like black walls, and he
had only his thoughts for company. They
were not cheerful. He scarcely knew what
to expect. Whether Dick would be alive or
dead, or, worse still, in a sad condition of
mind. To him bodily ill seemed nothing
compared with the lucidity of the intellectual
powers. The saddest sight on earth, he
thought, was the ravings of a man in delirium,
or the dodderings of feeble imbecility. Into
which of these states could Dick have fallen?
could the mysterious warning of the old
butler be meant to convey that the unfortunate young fellow in a moment of frenzy
had attempted to commit suicide? Such
were Bruce's dreary ponderings while the
driver walked his horse up every small hill
along the road, and spared the horse down
every incline, so that it was very late when
at last they reached the bailiff's house; the
driver, seeing a light at the back door, halted
there. The rain dripped from the eaves
and a big puddle intercepted the entrance,

but at the sound of wheels the door opened noiselessly, and the old butler appeared fully dressed with a candle in his hand.

"Ah, sir, thank God!" he said, "you've come, now all is well; you will be able to do more than I can. I am only a poor old man and a servant, but I feel love, sir, and dutifullest respect to the young master, and ah, sir, I have wished for you. Let me pay the fly, sir, don't you trouble, but step in here."

"In here" was the pantry where the old man had carefully ranged his plate on the few shelves it contained, and, the evening being damp, had lit a small fire and placed a kettle on the hob. Bruce walked in as he was desired and warmed his hands at the fire. He was a little chilled by the long drive and his own anxiety, and he found the cosy blaze most welcome. The old butler having dismissed the fly, now entered and bustled about, talking all the time. "Here, sir, I've got some sherry and sandwiches for you. I expected you to-night, and, thinks I, the poor gentleman will be hungry; and now you've come, please God, Mister Dick will soon be well again."

"I do not understand." To satisfy the

old man Bruce took a seat and proceeded to
drink some of the sherry. "What is the
matter with your master?"

"Matter, sir! everything is the matter,
he is shut up, so that none of us who love
him can get near; that viper, that aunt of
his, nurses him; it's *my* belief *she* drinks the
brandy and gives him only water, and
starves him until, in short, it's downright
murder."

"Perhaps she will not admit me."

"She dare not refuse, sir; you're a gentleman and master's friend, and we're only
servants. She's never tired of telling us so
either."

"At any rate you must take me to him;
shall we go upstairs now?"

"Yes, sir—yes; don't let's lose a minute.
Who knows but she may be murdering him
at this instant."

Bruce was sober and clearheaded, and he
was able to make allowances for the old
man's evident fear and flurry; yet even he
could not resist the impression that there
was something mysterious in this dark and
silent house, where a sick person lay, unseen
and unheard save by the woman who had

always shown herself his enemy. He followed the old butler cautiously up the narrow wooden stairs, his guide holding the candle and letting its light fall on the heavy beams, which, without careful treading, might have knocked against his head. At the top of the stairs they turned to the right, went down a small passage, stumbled up two or three stairs, and finally groped their way by the light of the flaring candle; gusts of wind swept along, nearly extinguishing it occasionally, and it seemed to Bruce once as if he felt the wings of a bat touch his face and skim past, bringing a quick current of cold air. Not a sound was to be heard but the cracking of the old woodwork and the gentle pattering of the rain against the passage window. Presently the old butler stopped before a door, put his ear to the keyhole to listen, holding his hand up as a warning to silence. Bruce waited breathlessly; in another instant he should know the worst. Having apparently satisfied himself that all was quiet, the butler turned the handle gently, and slipped into the room, motioning to Bruce to follow. A nightlight burnt on the washing-stand, and a nurse

slept, fully dressed, in an arm-chair. She
woke at the entrance of the newcomers, and
betrayed considerable surprise at the intru-
sion.

"It is an old friend of master's come to
nurse him," whispered the butler; "now,
nurse, if you want a bit of sleep you can go
and lie down."

"Yes, my good woman," said Bruce,
throwing anxious glances towards the bed,
where it seemed to him as if something
stirred. "You can safely leave your patient
to me; does he take medicine? what are
your directions?"

"He needs nothing just now, but something to drink if he wakes; there is the
lemonade, and he won't wake yet, I expect.
He has not long taken a sleeping-draught,"
said the nurse, too much bewildered by the
tone of quiet authority in which Bruce
spoke, to dare to dispute his orders, and
allowing herself to be led away passively
in search of much-desired rest by the butler.

"I will call you if anything is wanted,"
said Bruce, reassuringly.

The butler turned to whisper to him as he
went out. "It's all right now you're here;

don't you leave master, sir, on any account, and I shall feel he is safe in your hands."

The door closed, and Bruce was alone— alone in the small dark room with his un- conscious friend beginning at that instant to stir restlessly among the pillows.   He ap- proached the bed.   Dick's eyes were closed, and a cold-water bandage was tied round his head.   Yet he moved, and moved incessantly with the aimless wearying irritability of a fever patient.   Bruce stood and looked pity- ingly.   The fine strong young man reduced to such pitiable straits shocked him terribly.

" Dick," he said, stooping over him, and gently arranging his pillow.   The eyes did not unclose, and no shadow of memory or recognition passed over the pained features. Bruce drew a chair near the bedhead and watched more closely.   What stuff could Mrs. Vincent be made of that she had never summoned any of Dick's friends ?   Poor fellow, it was but too evident he had not long to live.   One wasted hand, the blue veins standing out strongly upon it, clutched at the counterpane, the other moved up and down beneath his head as though trying to ease the pain that tormented him.

Bruce had never watched by the sick bed of any one he loved before. His mother, though a martyr to rheumatism, seldom kept her room, and had never required his services. He was too much of a philosopher to fear death for himself, and would gladly have given his life in the cause of science or culture, yet his pity was strangely and deeply excited by the spectacle of his friend's pain and helplessness Once he had experienced, he remembered now to his shame, a moment of envy at the good fortune and the affection that attended Dick. Who was most to be envied now? Bruce with his sane intelligence and unimpaired power of work, or this poor young fellow the owner of wealth and estates, hopelessly consigned to sickness and death; and unconscious even of the love that noted each flicker of the eyelids. Suddenly the eyes opened wide, a vivid flush of colour came into the unshaven cheeks, the lips parted and a voice said " Luce."

Bruce almost started ; the sound was so hollow and unearthly and the man seemed so automatic. "It is I, your friend Julian," he said, tenderly, taking one of the poor hot hands in his. But the eyes closed again without a ray of consciousness, and the lips muttered unintelligibly.

Bruce sighed.

From side to side Dick moved with a kind of restless rythm, sometimes speaking, sometimes silent, breathing heavily, his brow seemingly on fire.

Bruce tried to distinguish what he was talking about, but could not catch the words, only it seemed to him as though again and again he heard the name "Luce" in all kinds of tones. The night passed more slowly than any night had ever passed before; he felt no inclination to slumber, no desire to relax for one moment the almost painful strain of attention; once or twice he presented the glass of lemonade to the invalid's lips, who drank, as he did all else, unconsciously and mechanically. And through the long slow hours, as the night-light sputtered, flared, and finally went out, and the grey dawn pierced gradually through the blinds, and threw a cold search-ing light around, that terrible undertone of incoherent, somnolent ravings, and mutter-ings, and broken whispers continued, rising and falling like the threatening surge of the sea. When morning came, Bruce saw more clearly the ravages the fever had wrought in his friend's countenance; hollow-eyed, drawn with pain, flushed with unnatural heat, and distorted by suffering, it was hard to recognise the features of the handsome man, who had looked out on life with a gay fearlessness. As soon as it was fairly light, Mrs. Vincent came in, dressed in a loose morning robe with a cup of some liquid in her hand. When she beheld Bruce she started violently, and almost dropped the cup.

"You here?" she said, adding almost fiercely, "Who sent for you?"

"I heard Dick was ill," answered Bruce, rising and greeting her respectfully; "and, as he is my dearest friend, I came to nurse him."

"Without communicating with me," she said more defiantly. Bruce made a little bow of acquiescence. Her anger increased.

"You have been guilty of a gross impertinence; you had better leave the house at once."

"I regret to annoy you, Madam, but I shall not leave my friend till he is better."

"You are insolent," she said, maddened out of all sense of self-control; "this is my house, I order you to go."

"It is Dick's bailiff's house, and he is master here; take care, don't speak so loud, you may disturb him, and quarrels in a sick man's room are most unseemly."

She threw a glance of hatred towards the bed.

"*He* won't hear, he doesn't know any one, he will never speak coherently again. You have come to nurse a *dead* man."

"Possibly. All the more reason why you should not object to my offering him the last services of which friendship is capable."

Both believed that it was as they said, there could be no hope for Dick. The London doctor had remarked to Mrs. Vincent, as he pocketed his heavy fee, and wrapped a comforter round his neck to guard himself from the damp on his way to the station, that "while there is life there is hope," but she was too good a nurse not to understand that this was a polite condemnation of the patient, and she took it so. She was enraged at Bruce's pertinacity, while at the same time his self-possession, and her conviction of his learning, overawed her. She reflected that no further harm or good could be done now, and she decided to dissimulate her rage, and to earn Bruce's good will by some show of attention.

"Well, if you choose to stay," she said, a little awkwardly (graciousness was at no time Mrs. Vincent's forte), "I suppose you had better, but you will find it very wearisome. He rambles so."

" What nourishment do you give him ? " asked Bruce, not noticing her semi-apology.

" He will take nothing but liquids, milk and a little beef tea," she said, holding out the cup for inspection.

" Thank you, I will see that he takes as much food as possible. You must have many duties to attend to. Leave the sick-room to me."

"Indeed! and pray how are *you* qualified?"

" By the power of love, madam, of disinterested affection, a pharmacopœia of which I daresay you have never heard."

Mrs. Vincent bit her thin lips. This man was not to be deceived. He was a clever

antagonist, and would unravel her little web
of intrigue. She more than ever regretted
to be forced to leave him with Dick, and yet
how could she prevent it, as he said it was
not her house—yet; if it were, she added
vindictively, such a fellow as he should
never darken her doors.

"Do you want anything," she asked,
determined to maintain a show of authority,
"shall I order a room for you?"

"I want nothing but freedom, and servants who will obey my orders. I presume
the nurse is trustworthy."

"Yes," muttered Mrs. Vincent meekly,
she was beginning to feel the power of a
strong and superior mind.

"Very well. As soon as the doctor comes,
I will see him, and will then give further
orders as they may be required." He took
the cup from Mrs. Vincent's unwilling hand,
and motioned to her to withdraw.

She would fain have resisted, but she felt
that her appearance with hair untidily
fastened up, and matronly form enveloped
in a loose flannel dressing-gown that had
seen its best day, and already become a
veteran in the cause of measles and other

diseases, was more or less unattractive, and that she was placed in a humiliating position. For her next contest of strength with this calm, cold man, she must find a better vantage ground. Mrs. Vincent despised dress, and yet was forced to acknowledge that an elderly woman in a faded flannel dressing-gown lacked most of the elements of impressiveness and authority. It was not for nothing that the Greeks made stately Juno wear long and flowing robes; drapery inspires respect if it does not always command admiration.

"Very well, I will leave him to you for the present, and when the doctor comes we will consult *together*."

She laid great stress on the word "together," and with this Parthian shot she wisely left the room.

Bruce stood still a moment, the cup in his hand. He looked critically at its unappetizing contents, put his finger in, and tasted a few drops. "Very nasty!" he thought. "No, I had better be on the safe side." Thus saying, he poured the cup-full of liquid away into the slop-pail, and rang the bell with a masterful air. Dick seemed to

be sleeping now, even the hot colloquy
between his aunt and his friend had not disturbed him. He lay quiet, and seemed to
breathe more easily.   Bruce walked to the
window, opened it, and gently raised the
blind. The sick room was stifling, but outside the morning broke fair and bright, a
delicious fragrance of flowers and damp
earth rose from the ground; the rain had
ceased, and everything rejoiced in its freshness. The cabbage-roses in the little garden
held glistening drops of dew in their pink
petals, and the spikes of the sweetbriar
hedge were studded as with diamonds.
The birds twittered and sang, and in the
distance a cock crowed lustily. Was it now,
perhaps for the first time, that Bruce found
leisure to admire a sunrise, and the gradual
splendid awakening into life of sleeping
nature ? He gazed for some time, a new
sense of pleasure stealing into his soul; a
pleasure, certainly not animal, but yet which
had no connection with the intellectual joys
he had hitherto found in books. Presently
he dropped the blind and came back to the
bed. Decidedly Dick was sleeping more

peacefully than before, and there was the ghost of a smile upon his lips. At that instant there came a knock at the door, and a servant, putting her head in, said, " If you please, sir, the doctor is come."

CHAPTER XIX.

THE doctor pronounced his patient somewhat better, though the condition of febrile
excitement he found, puzzled him.

"There is nothing in his state to produce
so much fever," he said; "I cannot help
thinking that it is rather connected with
mental than bodily troubles. Do you know
if he had any great trouble weighing on his
mind?"

Bruce thought for an instant. "None
I should say, absolutely none. He was a
most fortunate man in all his circumstances."

"Then I can't account for it; there must
be some lesion that I know nothing about.
Does he talk much; on what subjects does
his mind run?"

"He mutters and talks incessantly; but I
cannot distinguish the words."

"Then please pay great attention to whatever you do hear, and let me know."

"You do not anticipate any immediate danger?"

"Danger! There is great danger, but I anticipate no special evil consequences if we can keep up his strength and keep down the fever."

"I shall do my best."

"You are a great friend, I presume?" said the doctor, pulling out his watch. "There is nothing like careful nursing; we doctors can effect but little in a case of this sort. The nurse who is here is an excellent person, but it will do her no harm to be kept up to her work by a personal friend."

Then the doctor, who had his rounds to make and could not afford to waste precious time in pretty speeches, departed, and Bruce felt himself charged with all the onus of poor Dick's recovery.

Mental troubles, now what could they be? Dick's difficulties had lain hitherto chiefly in money embarrassments, but those were now removed, and at no time had such things seriously affected his spirits. It must be something far worse than this that disordered his brain and kept up an unceasing irritability. What could it be? Bruce was beginning to learn that life's problems are far more intricate and puzzling than the severest test in mathematics. When the premises are doubtful it is not easy to argue correctly. He pondered. Just then the sleeper turned more quickly, and, as Bruce bent down closer to catch the words uttered, he distinctly heard " Luce, oh my poor Luce ! " in tones of regretful anguish. " Luce ! " that had been the name then that he thought to distinguish before. " Luce ! " why should he call on her? Of course it was only the broken dream of a sick man, harking back upon the past memories of his life. Again he heard " Don't send me away, Luce. I am so hot and your hands are cool." Strange recollections these ! " Why will you be so unselfish? Let us go away—no one will know—Luce, oh Luce ! " and the passionate cry died away into a low moan. Bruce sat motionless. The doctor had bidden him gather the secret; he was merely obeying orders in Dick's own interest. " You said I did not love you, poor little Luce."

Bruce shrank together; could he be justified in listening to talk of this kind?

"And your eyes, oh, your eyes, do take them away, they burn me; why are you so angry? I did my best, indeed I did my best."

Then again Dick relapsed into silence and Bruce sat by thinking. What strange lapses of mind illness brought with it! why should Dick harp so constantly on Luce instead of dwelling rather on the perfections of Lady Fenchurch, the woman he had passionately loved? There was some rift within the lute, some misunderstanding; it could not be Luce's fault, he felt sure; to Bruce she was a goddess who could do no wrong, and yet not a goddess merely but the most charming and loveable of girls. He allowed himself to feel glad that Dick had not married her. They were ill-matched; even with all Bruce's affectionate infatuation for his friend he dared not think him worthy of so precious a jewel. The days passed. Bruce saw little of Mrs. Vincent; she came upstairs occasionally, looking cross and sour; she suggested this and found fault with that, and went down again more convinced than ever in her own mind, that Bruce's assiduity and superhuman attention would restore Dick to life. Bruce was beginning to look like a shadow himself, his hands grew more and more transparent, his face thinner, but the light in his eyes seemed to have transferred itself from within to without; a tender watchfulness guarded every movement, a solicitous anxiety provoked every comfort. Little by little Dick grew calmer, the touch of his friend's hand seemed to soothe and please him. He slept oftener and for longer intervals, and, when Bruce scanned his face with earnest eyes it seemed to him that a flash of recognition passed over the pale features. Again he looked, and this time he felt quite sure of it. A soft sigh unclosed the lips, and faint as a breath of summer air he caught the sound

"Julian, is it you?"

"It is I, Dick. Thank God you are better."

The waxen hand felt over the counterpane for his, and clasped it with the loving trust of gratitude. Then the tired head turned itself, and Dick slept again, like the wearied child that has said good-night to its mother,

and made its peace with all the world.
After that, every day a fresh stage towards
recovery was made. Dick spoke and moved,
though still languidly yet more naturally,
and began to converse with his friend in
quiet and cheerful tones. Bruce was
genuinely overjoyed. To him it was as
though he had suddenly emerged from some
dark tortuous cavern into the full light of
day. He had grieved so over Dick, with
the thread of his bright young life snapped
suddenly, and all the possibilities of develop-
ment and happiness cut short; that the
abrupt change in his previsions, the sudden
leap from darkling fears to vivid hope, left
him dazed and blinded, like a half-blind
prisoner in the brilliant gleams of unaccus-
tomed sunshine. He nursed Dick as tenderly
as any woman, pressed on his dainty appetite
the most delicate food, and humoured his
smallest wish. His long clumsy hands, that
hitherto held only voluminous folios, or note-
making pen and pencil, learnt a new handi-
ness. His strength was most acceptable in
lifting the poor invalid, whose weight had
sadly dwindled from the day he rowed stroke-
oar in the Cambridge boat, and his delicacy

of touch could not have been surpassed by
that of the most skilled surgeon. The nurse
found her services almost dispensed with,
and began to ramble about the fields and
bring home bunches of wild flowers, which,
after a long period of pent-up existence in a
town hospital, seemed to her supernaturally
beautiful. Bruce, himself, rarely stirred
from the sick room. He would sit for hours
reading, while Dick slept, ready to jump up
at the smallest sound; he had even deprived
himself voluntarily of his pipe, lest the smell
of tobacco should incommode the fastidious
invalid. Not the least of his self-denial was
comprised in the scarcity of books to which
he cheerfully resigned himself, a volume of
Alexander Barclay's " Ship of Fules " being
the only literature he had carried away from
his lodgings. Perhaps, next to the Bible,
the " Ship of Fules " is as good food for the
mind of a man cast up on the dry shore of
involuntary idleness as any other. Thence
he can view the follies, and ugliness, and
misery of the steaming hurrying waves of
the world below at his ease, and moralise in
the luxury of security.

The fools that get and the fools that give,

the fools that lie and the fools that waste; who has not known some, and pitied others, and suffered under the remainder? And, as the scholar pored over the pages adorned with droll and grotesque woodcuts, his spirit grew calm and resigned. Luce was his beacon-star, but only a star, intangible and afar off.

While Bruce thus steeped his mind in the sweets of study, and sought to reduce passion to its divinest element, the element of respectful worship, he noticed with surprise that Dick's recovery proceeded very slowly. The great and beneficial change that had appeared at first did not maintain itself, and seemed to give place to a stationary condition. Dick's sleep was fairly good, his appetite tolerable, and yet he did not improve. He had moments of intense and unreasonable depression, he would turn and start and cry out in his sleep, and lie for hours with his eyes fixed on a particular spot in the wall-paper, as though he had neither strength nor inclination for more. Bruce thought again of the mental troubles, and one day he ventured to speak.

" Dick, my boy," he said, sitting very

near him and watching his face carefully,
"what is the matter with you? where are
your old spirits?"

"How can a fellow have any spirits after
such a confounded illness as mine? When I
can use my limbs and get about I shall be
all right."

"Dick, why don't you confide in me?
why dont you tell me your secrets?—perhaps
I could help you; I am sure you are unhappy."

"No, I'm only bored, and so must you be,
Julian. I declare you never go out; why
don't you take a walk?"

"You are trying to evade my question;
you look troubled, it is more than pain that
worries you."

Dick's brow puckered. He was silent a
minute, then he said, "I see I was wrong,
Julian, we can't live our own lives—and I
know it now it's too late."

"How too late?"

"I'm an unlucky devil," his voice grew
hard and bitter, "everything I touch goes
wrong."

"Dick, you are a little unjust—at least,
you have faithful friends."

"1 know." Dick took Bruce's hand and wrung it. "It's no good talking—by-the-bye, did I rave in my delirium ?— one talks such infernal nonsense at those times."

"You did talk," confessed Bruce, measuring out his confidences with his eye on Dick, as a doctor feels his patient's pulse. "You talked chiefly of one person —— "

"Of one person —— "

"By which I conclude that person was dear to you."

"Not a bit of it, that does not follow at all."

"Strangely enough, her name seems to be Luce."

Dick coloured violently. "What a fool a man is when he is ill !"

"A fool ? that is a matter of opinion. Tell me what is there between you and Miss Windermere ?"

"There is nothing. I dare say she was right; she made me pay the penalty of my own folly; she would not marry me, you know. I told her I did not care for her." His tones were hurried and angry and broken, and the flush in his face continued.

"And you—love her now." Bruce spoke

with calm precision, but every word seemed like a knife cutting into his heart. His pearl, his precious one—how could he bear to talk of her thus? He was like a man in a dream assisting at his own execution.

"Yes," Dick said, dreamily, the flush dying away, "I suppose I do. I am always thinking of her now; she was the only un-selfish woman I ever met, and I can't forget her."

"Why don't you try?"

"Oh, what does it matter?—if I could only see her once—whenever I shut my eyes her face haunts me, it is full of reproach, and oh! so sad—and sometimes I think she is quite near, and she seems kind, and then I wake and it is only a delusion."

"And then you cry out and have wakeful nights, and the fever goes on."

"Yes," Dick sighed, "and there is nothing to be done. Go on reading, this is idle talk."

Bruce closed his book, keeping one finger between the leaves. "No, I think I will talk a little longer about these strange fancies of yours. Do you think if you saw her and could speak to her, you would be happier."

" Yes, it is funny, isn't it ? you know that I am such a matter-of-fact chap, and I keep feeling as if I wanted her to forgive me—I behaved awfully bad to her."

" Perhaps she would not like to see you." Bruce rose and walked to the window.

" Oh, she would—I am certain she loves me still—and she is so unselfish."

Bruce stood with his back to the bed. His lips quivered, but he was determined to show no emotion. Dick must never guess his secret. He remained silent a moment.

" What is the matter, Julian ? " said the voice from the bed. " Do you think me a fool, why don't you answer ? "

" I don't think a man is a fool who loves wisely and well," said Julian, in somewhat shaky tones, but he did not turn his head. With a swift rush came swooping down upon him the great temptation of his life, hurrying him to a decision, holding him to his choice as between the grip of a sharp pair of pincers. He had learnt the meaning of many things, he had studied deeply in the book of history, he was now to learn the meaning of friendship, to be instructed in the deepest recoils of the human heart. He stood at the window and idly watched the girl gathering lavender sprigs in the garden. Lavender, to put away among precious stored-up things, to give a sweet odour of the bygone summer and leave a lingering memory of warmth and life. Lavender! So be it. He turned to the bed. His face was very pale and his teeth were tightly closed. "Dick, my boy," he said, trying to speak cheerfully, "you musn't be so morbid; all this will conduce to your happiness, I am sure; now lie down and try to get a sleep. To-morrow I am going for a long walk. You are nearly well now, and don't require me."

CHAPTER XX.

" THAT is not the way," said Dick, as the nurse in Bruce's absence tried to re-arrange his pillows, "I like my head higher." He pushed feebly with his hand and sank back exhausted. " Never mind, that will do." The nurse, believing that the heat had made her patient fractious, forbore to press the matter, and retired into a corner with her sewing. The day had been sultry, black thundery clouds swept over the sky, and not a breath stirred the leaves, a sullen hush covered all things, and in Dick's small room, even with the window wide open and the Venetian blinds closed, the air was oppressive to suffocation. He had been alone with the nurse all day; he missed his friend's company extremely, and cherished a kind of angry bitterness at being thus deserted. He

had tried to be cheerful, but now he was
only hot and tired and nervously depressed.
Like the horse in his weary mill-round his
thoughts ran their usual circle; he pictured
Luce to himself as she stood beside him that
spring morning when they parted, with the
faint sweet smell of the violets and prim-
roses around and the dew-laden sprays touching their foreheads. His fancy ran riot, he
remembered the warmth of her kisses, and
the deep love in her voice. He remembered
how carelessly he had accepted that great
gift and how angrily he had left her. Where
was she now; was he forgiven? A slight
rustling noise startled him, the nurse got up
and went to the door, which was hidden
from him by a screen.

"Nurse, what is it?" he heard her return,
and shut his eyes wearily, trying to keep
his dream of that fair spring morning;
"what is it? I don't want anything."

A soft cool hand was laid gently on his
impatient fingers, and a breath of the sweet-
scented spring air seemed wafted over him.
He opened his eyes, surprised and somewhat less irritable, and met Luce's soft and
earnest glances.

"Luce, you here, why—am I dreaming—oh! if you are a dream—don't leave me, don't," he said, stretching out his hands.

"I am no dream, Dick—look at me."

Then he timidly took her hand again, feasting his starving eyes on her dear blushing face—fascinated, soothed. Forgetting all but that she was near, he drew her slowly, closer, closer, down towards him, till her cool, fragrant lips rested on his hot, parched mouth.

"Luce, my little love, the one unselfish woman in the world." Then he put her away a little and looked at her. Luce did not speak, but happiness shone in her shining glances, and love played about the sensitive corners of her smiling mouth.

"It is too good to be true—did I summon you by wishes, dear?"

"Mr. Bruce summoned me," said Luce, slipping down beside the bed on her knees, and laying her cheek bashfully on Dick's hand. "I came at his request."

"Dear good fellow, where is he? I should like to thank him."

"I want no thanks," said Bruce, approaching from his hiding-place behind the

curtain, "but I have something to give you."
As he spoke he handed him a letter and a
small case wrapped in white paper.

"The necklace!" cried Dick; "where
was it found?"

"Mrs. Vincent had it in her dressing-case;
she stole it from you, and in rescuing her
jewels from the fire you rescued it also, and
saved your own reputation."

Dick could not speak. The surprise and
gratitude he felt almost choked him.

"And this letter," he tore it open with
feverish anxiety, read, and handed it to
Bruce.

"Free!" he said, leaning back satisfied
on his pillows; "thank God, *free!*"

The letter was from Lady Fenchurch,
releasing him from his engagement.

"I know," she said, "that you have
ceased to love me; and, as I find Mr. Peter
Fenchurch a most charming person, and he
is anxious to marry me, it will be more con-
venient and agreeable to all if I return you
your word, and tell you, you are free."

Bruce read without speaking, folded the
letter, and glanced towards the bed.

Luce's little brown head lay pillowed in

Dick's arms, as he bent over her, with an expression of rapt happiness shining in his eyes. "My love," he said, in a low voice, "my little love, kiss me; now indeed I believe in a good woman's heart."

Bruce turned away. He dared not break the silence of this solemn moment, but a swallow flying past the window at that instant might have seen that his face was pale, and down the haggard white cheek a great tear rolled. For he had dreamed a dream; he had conversed with a vision of infinite bliss, and seen opening vistas of irradiating light. But the light had faded into darkness, and the angels had soared aloft as he closed for ever the glowing pages of the book of life and love, and turned himself again, a cold and solitary man, to the stern uncompromising black-letter of duty and self-sacrifice.

THE END.

www.ingramcontent.com/pod-product-compliance
Lightning Source LLC
Chambersburg PA
CBHW030628030726
47497CB00006B/1691